AWAKENED BY THE
SCARRED ITALIAN

AWAKENED BY THE SCARRED ITALIAN

ABBY GREEN

MILLS & BOON

First published in Great Britain 2019
by Mills & Boon, an imprint of HarperCollins*Publishers*
1 London Bridge Street, London, SE1 9GF

Large Print edition 2019

© 2019 Abby Green

ISBN: 978-0-263-08307-1

MIX
Paper from
responsible sources
FSC™ C007454

This book is produced from independently certified FSC™ paper to ensure responsible forest management. For more information visit www.harpercollins.co.uk/green.

Printed and bound in Great Britain
by CPI Group (UK) Ltd, Croydon, CR0 4YY

This is for Sharon Kendrick,
whose advice I *should* have taken
about two months before I did.

I got there in the end!

Thanks, Sharon!

CHAPTER ONE

LARA TEMPLETON WAS glad of the delicate black lace obscuring her vision and hiding her dry eyes from the sly looks of the crowd around the open grave. They might well suspect that she wasn't grieving the death of her husband, the not so Honourable Henry Winterborne, but she didn't want to give them the satisfaction of confirming it for themselves. So she kept herself hidden. Dressed in sober black from head to toe, as befitting a widow.

A grieving widow who had been left nothing by her husband. Who had, in fact, been little more than an indentured slave for the last three months. A detail this crowd of jackals would no doubt crow over if it ever became public knowledge.

Her husband had had good reason to leave her with nothing. She wouldn't have wanted his money anyway. It wasn't why she'd married him, no matter what people believed. And he hadn't left her anything because she hadn't given him what he wanted. *Herself.* It was her fault he'd ended up injured and in a wheelchair for the duration of their marriage.

No, it wasn't your fault. If he hadn't tried to—

Lara's churning thoughts skittered to a halt when she realised that people were looking at her expectantly. The back of her neck prickled.

The priest gave a discreet cough and said, *sotto voce*, 'If you'd like to throw some soil on the coffin now, Mrs Winterborne...'

Lara flinched inwardly at the reference to her married name. The marriage had been a farce, and she'd only agreed to it because she'd been blackmailed into it by her uncle. She saw a trowel on the ground near the edge of the grave and, even though it was the last thing she wanted to do, because she felt like a hypocrite, she bent down and scooped up some earth before letting it fall onto the coffin. It made a hollow-sounding *thunk.*

For a moment she had the nonsensical notion that her husband might reach out from the grave and pull her in with him, and she almost stumbled forward into the empty space.

There was a gasp from the crowd and the priest caught her arm to steady her.

Unbelievable, thought the man standing nonchalantly against a tree nearby with his arms crossed over a broad chest. He fixed his gaze on the widow, but she didn't look his way once. She was too busy acting the part—practically throwing herself into the grave.

His mouth firmed, its sensual lines drawing into one hard flat one. He had to hand it to her. She played the part well, dressed in a black form-fitting dress that clung to her willowy graceful frame. Her distinctive blonde hair was tied back in a low bun and a small circular hat sat on her head with a gauzy veil obscuring her face. Oh, he had no doubt she was genuinely grieving…but not for her husband. For the fortune she hadn't been left.

The man's mouth curved up into a cruel smile. That was the least Lara Winterborne, née Templeton, deserved.

The back of Lara's neck prickled again. But this time it prickled with heat. Awareness.

Something she hadn't felt in a long time. She looked up, shaking off the strange sensation, relieved to see that people were moving away from the grave, talking in low tones. It was over.

A movement in the distance caught her eye and she saw the tall figure of a man, broad and powerful, walking away towards the cars. He wore a cap and what looked like a uniform. Just one of the drivers.

But something about his height and those broad shoulders snagged her attention…the way he walked with loose-limbed athleticism. More than her attention. For a fleeting moment she felt dizzy because he reminded her of… *No.* She shut down the thought immediately. It couldn't be him.

Snippets of nearby whispered conversation distracted Lara from the stranger, and as much as she tried to tune it out some words couldn't be unheard.

'Is it really true? She gets nothing?'
'Never should have married her…'
'She was only trying to save her reputation

after almost marrying one of the world's most notorious playboys...'

That last comment cut far too close to her painful memories, but Lara had become adept at disregarding snide comments over the past two years. Contrary to what these people believed, she couldn't be more relieved that she'd been left with not a cent of Winterborne's fortune.

She would never have married him in a million years if she hadn't been faced with an impossible situation. A heinous betrayal by her uncle. Nevertheless, she wasn't such a monster that she couldn't feel some emotion for Winterborne's death. But mostly she felt empty. Weary. Tainted by association.

The grief she *did* feel was for something else entirely. Something that had been snatched away from her before it had ever had a chance to live and breathe. *Someone*. Someone she'd loved more than she'd ever thought it possible to love another human being. He'd been hurt and tortured because of her. He'd almost died. She'd had no choice but to do what she had to save him further pain and possibly worse.

Swallowing back the constriction in her throat, Lara finally turned away from the grave and started to walk towards where just a couple of cars remained. She wasn't paying for any of this. She couldn't afford it. As soon as she returned to the exclusive apartment she'd shared with her husband there would be staff waiting with her bags to escort her off the premises. Her husband had wanted to maintain the façade as far as the graveside. But now all bets were off. She was on her own.

She clamped down on the churning panic in her gut. She would deal with what to do and where to go when she had to.

That's in approximately half an hour, Lara!

She ignored the inner voice.

One of the funeral directors was standing by the back door of her car, holding it open. She saw the shadowy figure of the driver in the front seat. Once again she felt that prickle of recognition but she told herself she was being silly, superstitious. She was only thinking of *him* now because she was finally free of the burden that had been thrust upon her. But she couldn't allow her thoughts to go there.

She murmured her thanks as she sat into the back of the luxurious car. It was the last bit of decadence she'd experience for some time. Not that she cared. A long time ago, when she'd lost her parents and her older brother in a tragic accident, she'd learnt the hard way that nothing external mattered once you'd lost the people you loved most.

But clearly it hadn't been enough of a lesson to protect her from falling in love with—

The car started moving and Lara welcomed the distraction.

Not thinking of him now.

No matter how much a random stranger had reminded her of him.

Unable to stop her curiosity, though, she looked at the only part of the driver's face she could see in the rear-view mirror. It was half hidden by aviator-style sunglasses, but she could see a strong aquiline nose and firm top lip. A hard, defined jaw.

Her heart started to beat faster, even though rationally she knew it couldn't possibly be—

At that moment he seemed to sense her regard

from the back and she saw his arm move before the privacy window slid up. Cutting her off.

For some reason Lara felt as if he'd put the window up as a rebuke. *Ridiculous*. He was just a driver! He'd probably assumed she wanted some privacy...

Still, the disquieting niggle wouldn't go away.

It got worse when she realised that while they were headed in the right direction, back to the Kensington apartment she'd shared with her husband, they weren't getting closer. They were veering off the main high street onto another street nearby, populated by tall, exclusive town-houses.

Lara had walked down this street nearly every day for two years, and had relished every second she wasn't in the oppressively claus-trophobic apartment with her husband. But it wasn't her street. The driver must be mistaken.

As the car drew to a stop outside one of the houses Lara leant forward and tapped the win-dow. For a moment nothing happened. She tapped again, and suddenly it slid down with a mechanical buzz.

The driver was still facing forward, his left

hand on the wheel. For some reason Lara felt nervous. Yet she was on a familiar street with people passing by the car.

'Excuse me, we're not in the right place. I'm just around the corner, on Marley Street.'

Lara saw the man's jaw clench, and then he said, 'On the contrary, *cara.* We're in exactly the right place.'

That voice. *His voice.*

Lara's breath stopped in her throat and in the same moment the man took off the cap and removed his sunglasses and turned around to face her.

She wasn't sure how long she sat there, stupefied. In shock. Time ceased to exist as a linear thing.

His words from two years ago were still etched into her mind. *'You will regret this for the rest of your life, Lara. You belong to me.'*

And here he was to crow over her humiliation.

Ciro Sant'Angelo.

The fact that she'd said to him that day, *'I will regret nothing,'* was not a memory she relished. She'd regretted it every second since that day. But she'd been desperate, and she'd had no choice. He'd been brutalised and almost killed. And all because she'd had the temerity to meet him and fall in love, going against the very exacting plans her uncle had orchestrated on her behalf, unbeknownst to her.

If she was honest with herself, she'd dreamed of this moment. That Ciro would come for her. But the reality was almost too much to take in. She wasn't prepared. She would never be prepared for a man like Ciro Sant'Angelo. She hadn't been two years ago and she wasn't now.

Panic surged. She blindly reached for the door handle but it wouldn't open. She tried the other one. *Locked.* Breathless, she looked back at him and said, 'Open the doors, Ciro, this is crazy.'

But nothing happened. He responded with a sardonic twist of his mouth. 'Should I be flattered that you remember me, Lara?'

She might have laughed at that moment if she hadn't been so stunned. Ciro Sant'Angelo was not a man easily forgotten by anyone. Tall, broad and leanly muscular, he oozed charisma and authority. Add to that the stunning symmetry of a face dominated by deep-set dark eyes and a mouth sculpted for sin. A hard jaw and slightly hawkish profile cancelled out any prettiness.

He would have been perfection personified if it wasn't for the jagged white ridge of skin that ran from under his right eye to his jaw. She could only look at it now with sick horror as the knowledge sank into her gut: she was responsible for that brutal scar.

He angled the right side of his face towards her, a hard light in his eyes. 'Does it disgust you?'

She shook her head slowly. It didn't detract from his beauty, it added a savage element. Dangerous.

'Ciro…' Lara said faintly now, as the truth finally sank in, deep in her gut. This wasn't a dream or a mirage…or a nightmare. She shook her head. 'What are you doing here? What do you want?'

I want what's mine.

The words beat through Ciro Sant'Angelo's body like a Klaxon. His blood was up, boiling over.

Lara Templeton—*Winterborne*—was here. Within touching distance. After two long years. Years in which he'd tried and failed to excise her treacherous, beautiful face from his mind.

A face he needed to see now more than he needed to acknowledge her question. 'Take your hat off.'

Her bright blue eyes flashed behind the veil. He could see the slope of her cheek down to that delicate jaw and the mouth that had made him want to sin as soon as he'd laid eyes on it. Full and ripe. A sensual reminder that beneath her elegant and coolly blonde exterior she was all fire.

Her lips compressed for a second and then she lifted a trembling hand—*another nice dramatic touch*—and pulled off the hat and veil.

And even though Ciro had steeled himself to face her once again she took his breath away. She hadn't changed in two years. She was still a classic beauty. Finely etched eyebrows framing huge blue eyes ringed with long dark lashes... High cheekbones and a straight nose... And that mouth... Like a crushed rosebud. Promising decadence even as her eyes sent a message of innocence and naivety.

He'd fallen for it. Badly. Almost fatally.

'Not here,' he said curtly, angry with himself for letting Lara get to him on a level that he'd hoped to have under control. 'We'll talk inside.'

Inside where? Lara was about to ask, but Ciro was already out of the car and striding towards an intimidating townhouse. Her door was opened by a uniformed man—presumably the real driver?—and Lara didn't have much choice but to step out of the back of the car.

As she did, she noticed two or three intimidating-looking men in suits with ear-pieces. *Security.* Of course. Ciro had always been cavalier about his safety before, but she could imagine that after the kidnapping he'd changed.

The kidnapping.

A cold shiver went down her spine. Ciro Sant'Angelo had been kidnapped and bru-tally assaulted two years ago. Lara had been kidnapped with him, but she'd been released within hours. Dumped at the side of a road out-side Florence. It had been the singularly most terrifying thing they'd ever experienced and *she'd* been the reason it had happened.

For a moment Lara hesitated at the bottom of the steps leading up to a porch and an open front door. She could see black and white tiles in the circular hallway. A grand-looking interior.

'Mr Sant'Angelo is waiting.'

One of the suited men was extending his arm towards the house. He looked civil enough, but she imagined it was a very superficial civility.

She went up the steps and through the door. A sleek-looking middle-aged woman approached her with a polite smile. 'Miss Templeton, welcome. Please let me take your things. Mr Sant'Angelo is waiting for you in the lounge.'

Numbly, Lara handed over her hat and bag, barely even noticing the use of her maiden name. She wore a light cape-style coat over her shift dress and she left it on, even though it was warm. She followed the woman, not liking the sensation that she was walking into the lion's den.

The sensation was only heightened when she saw the tall figure of Ciro, his back to her as he helped himself to a drink from a tray on the far side of the room.

'Would you like tea or coffee, Miss Templeton?'

Lara shook her head at the question from the woman and murmured, 'No, thanks.' The housekeeper left the room.

The muted sounds of London traffic could be heard through the huge windows. It was a palatial lounge, beautifully decorated in classic colours with massive paintings hanging on the walls. The paintings were abstract, and a vivid memory exploded into Lara's head of when Ciro had taken her to an art gallery in Florence, after hours.

They'd only just met a few days previously, and she'd been surprised enough at his choice of gallery to make him say with a mocking smile, 'You expected a rough Sicilian to have no taste?'

She'd blushed, because he'd exposed her for assuming that a very alpha Italian man would veer towards something more...classical, conservative.

She'd turned to him, still shy around him,

wondering what on earth he was doing with her, a pale English arts student. 'You're not rough…not at all.'

He'd been like a sleek panther, oozing a very lethal sense of coiled sensual energy.

The gallery had been hushed and reverential. She could still remember the delicious knot of tension deep in her abdomen, and how she'd thought to herself, *How can I not fall in love with this man who opens art galleries especially for me and makes me feel more alive than I've ever felt?*

They hadn't even kissed at that stage…

Ciro's voice broke through her reverie. 'Would you like something stronger, Lara? Perhaps some brandy for the overwhelming grief you must be feeling?'

Lara's nerves were jangling. He'd turned to face her now, and she noticed that he'd taken off the jacket and wore dark trousers and a white shirt open at the throat. Her mouth went dry. She knew how he tasted there. She could still remember how she'd explored that hollow with her tongue—

Stop.

She ignored his question. 'How long have you lived here?' Had he been here all this time? Just seconds away from where she'd been existing so miserably?

Lara thought she saw Ciro's hand tighten on his glass, but put it down to her overwrought imagination. He said, 'I bought it months ago but the renovations have only just been completed.'

So he hadn't been living here. Somehow that thought comforted Lara. She didn't know if she could have borne being married to Winterborne while knowing Ciro was so close. Even the thought of seeing him with another woman coming out of this house made her insides clench. *Crazy.* She had no jurisdiction over this man. She never had. She'd been dreaming. Delusional.

She lifted her chin. 'I don't have time for this, Ciro...whatever it is that you want. I have to be somewhere.'

Evicted. She ignored the fresh spiking of panic.

Ciro lifted his tumbler of golden liquid and

downed the lot in one go. For a second Lara wished she'd asked for a drink.

Then he said slowly, 'But that's just it, Lara. You don't have anywhere to go, do you?'

She actually felt the blood drain from her face. How could he possibly…?

'How can I know?'

He read her mind. Speared her with that dark gaze. Maybe she'd spoken out loud. She felt as if she were slipping under water, losing all sense of control.

He lifted a brow. 'The guests at the funeral were a hotbed of gossip, but I also have my contacts, who've informed me that Winterborne left everything to a distant relative and that as soon as you collect your things from the apartment, you're out on the streets. As for your trust fund—apparently you've blown through that too. Poor penniless Lara. You should have stayed with me. I'm worth three times as much as your dead husband and you wouldn't have had to put up with an old man in your bed for the past two years.'

Lara's head hurt to think of how he'd obtained all that information about her trust fund, and her insides churned at the mention of *old man.*

Any money left to her by her parents had been long gone before she'd ever had a chance to lay her hands on it. 'It was never about the money.'

Ciro's mouth tightened. 'No. It was about class.'

No, Lara thought, *it was about blackmail and coercion.*

But, yes, it had been about class too. Albeit not for her; she couldn't have cared less about class. She never had. Not that Ciro would ever believe her. Not after the way she'd convinced him otherwise.

She clamped her lips together, resisting the urge to defend herself when she knew it would be futile. She hardly knew this person in front of her, even though at one time she'd felt as if she'd known every atom of his being. He'd disabused her of that romantic notion two years ago. Yet, she couldn't deny the rapid and persistent spike in her pulse-rate ever since Ciro had revealed himself. Her body *knew* him.

Something caught her eye then, and she

gasped. His right hand…the one holding the glass…was missing a little finger.

He saw where her gaze had gone. 'Not very pretty, eh?'

Lara felt sick. She remembered Ciro lying in that hospital bed, his head and half his face covered in bandages…his arms… She'd been too distraught to notice much else.

'They did that to you? The kidnappers?' Her voice was a thread.

He nodded. 'It amused them. They got bored, waiting for their orders.'

Lara realised that he was different. Harder. More intimidating. 'Why am I here, Ciro?'

'Because you betrayed me.' He carefully put down the glass on the silver tray. And then he looked at her. 'And I'm here to collect my due.'

My due. The words revolved sickeningly in Lara's head.

'I don't owe you anything.' The words felt cumbersome in her mouth.

Liar, whispered a voice.

'Yes, Lara you do. You walked out on me when I needed you most, leaving me at the mercy of the press, who had a field day reviving all the old stories about my family's links to the Mafia. Not only that, you left me without a bride.'

A spark of anger mixed with her guilt as she recalled the lurid headlines in the aftermath of the kidnapping and her subsequent engagement to Henry Winterborne. She focused on the anger.

'You only wanted to marry me to take advantage of my connections to a society that had refused you access.'

Ciro hadn't loved her. He'd wanted her because at first she'd intrigued him, with her naivety and innocence, and then because of her connections and her name.

Over the last two years, with the benefit of distance and hindsight, Lara had come to acknowledge how refreshing someone like her must have been for someone as jaded as him. She'd been so trusting. *Loving.*

If they had married it never would have lasted. Not beyond the point where her allure would have worn off and he would have become disenchanted with her innocence. Not beyond the point at which her name and connections would have served their purpose for his ambitions. Of that she had no doubt.

Of course he wasn't going to forgive her for taking all that away from him. He was out for revenge.

For a heady moment Lara imagined telling him exactly what had happened. How events had conspired to drive them apart. How her uncle had so cruelly manipulated her. She even opened her mouth—but then she remembered Ciro's caustic words. They resounded in her head as if he'd said them only moments ago.

'Don't delude yourself that I felt anything more for you than you felt for me, Lara. I wanted you, yes, but that was purely physical. More than all of that I wanted you because marrying you would have given me a stamp of respectability that money can't buy.'

Ciro's voice broke through the toxic memory as he said coolly, 'I prefer to think of it as a kind of debt repayment. You said you'd marry me and I'm holding you to that original commitment. I need a wife, and I've no intention of getting into messy emotional entanglements when you're so convenient.'

Lara's blood drained south. 'That's the most ridiculous thing I've ever heard.'

'Is it? Really? People have married for a lot less, Lara.'

She looked at him helplessly, torn between hating him for appearing like a magician to turn her world upside down and desperately wanting to defend herself. But she'd lost that chance when she'd informed him coldly that she'd never had any intention of going through with their marriage because she was already promised to someone else—someone eminently more suitable.

She'd told him that it had amused her to go along with his whirlwind proposal, just to see him make a fool of himself over a woman he could never hope to marry. She'd told him all her breathy words of love had been mere platitudes.

She'd never forget the look of pure loathing that had come over his face after she'd spoken those bilious words. That had been the moment when she'd realised how deluded she'd been. And on some level she'd been glad she was playing a role, that at least she knew how he'd really felt.

He was almost killed because of you.

Lara felt sick again. He hadn't deserved that just for not loving her. And he hadn't deserved her lies. He'd saved her from the kidnappers. He'd offered up his life for hers. And then she'd learned she'd never really been in danger. He didn't know that, though. And right now the thought of him ever finding that out made her break out in a cold sweat. However much he hated her already, he would despise her even more.

Suddenly a ball of emotion swelled inside her chest. Lara couldn't bear it that Ciro thought so badly of her, even if it *was* her fault that she'd convinced him so well. Seeing him again was ripping open a raw wound inside her, and before she knew what she was doing she took a step forward, words tumbling out of her mouth.

'Ciro, I *did* want to marry you—more than anything. But my uncle…he was crazy…he'd lost everything. He didn't want me to marry you—he saw you as unworthy of a Templeton.

He forced me to say those awful things… They were all lies.'

Lara stopped abruptly and her words hung in the air. The atmosphere was thick with tension. Taut like a wire. Ciro was expressionless. She could remember a time when he'd used to look at her with such warmth and indulgence. And *love*, or so she'd thought. But it hadn't been love. It had been desire. Physical desire and the desire for success.

He lifted his hands and did a slow and deliberate hand-clap, the sound loud in the room. Lara flinched.

He shook his head. 'You really are something, Lara, you know that? But the victim act doesn't suit you and it's wasted on me. You really expect me to believe you were *coerced* into marrying a man old enough to be your father and rich enough to pay off the national debt of a small country? You forget I've seen your extensive repertoire of guises, and this innocent, earnest one is overdone and totally unnecessary.'

Her belly sank. She'd known it was futile to try. How could she explain how her uncle had manipulated and exploited her for his own gain since the moment he'd taken over her guardianship after her parents had died? The extent of his ruthlessness still shocked her, even now.

And she should recognise ruthlessness by now. She should have known Ciro hadn't been making idle threats two years ago. After all, he was Sicilian through every fibre of his being. He came from a long and bloody tradition of men who meted out revenge and punishment as a way of life, even if they had tried to distance themselves from all that in recent generations.

Ciro had told her once that his ancestors had been Moorish pirates and she could well believe it. She could see that he'd been wounded beyond redemption—not in his heart, because that had never been available to wound, but in his fierce Sicilian pride. Wounded when she'd walked away, and by the ruthless kidnappers when they'd physically altered him for ever and demonstrated that even he wasn't invincible.

She did owe him a debt. But it was a debt she couldn't afford to pay emotionally.

Lara's sense of self-preservation kicked in and she cursed herself for even trying to defend herself. She couldn't bear for him to find out just how vulnerable she really was—how nothing had really moved on for her since she'd known him. How the last two years of her life had been a kind of lonely torture.

She ruthlessly pushed aside all those memories and shrugged one shoulder minutely, affecting an air of boredom. She'd played this part once before—she could do it again.

'Well, it's been interesting to see you again, Ciro. But quite frankly you're even more pathetic now than you were two years ago, if this is how little you've moved on. What would you have done if Henry hadn't died? Kidnapped me? Seduced me away and then meted out your punishment?'

Lara's words fell like stinging barbs onto Ciro's skin. They cut far too close to the bone. He had been keeping tabs on her. Getting reports on her whereabouts and her activities— which, as far as he could see, had consisted of not much at all. Not even socialising. Her husband had monopolised her attention, kept her all to himself.

Ciro hadn't articulated to himself exactly what he was going to do where Lara was concerned, but he'd known he had reached some kind of nadir when he'd bought this house, sight unseen, because it was around the corner from where she lived. He'd known that he was reaching a place where he simply could not go on without exacting retribution.

Without seeing her again.

He crushed that rogue thought.

In the past few months, as a restless tension had increased inside him, he'd found himself contemplating seducing Lara Winterborne. He'd told himself it would be to prove just how duplicitous she was. But he knew that his motivations were murkier than that. Embedded in a place he'd locked them away two years ago, when she'd morphed into a stranger in front of his very eyes.

When she'd shown him up as a fool who had cast aside his well-worn cynical shell in a fit of blind lust and something even more disturbing. *Emotion.* A yearning for a life he'd never known. For a woman who was pure and who would be faithful. Loving. Loyal. A good mother. Fantasies he'd never indulged in before he'd met Lara and she'd exposed a seam of vulnerability he'd never acknowledged before.

The fact that he'd even considered seducing her away from her husband was galling for a man who had always vowed to conduct his life with more integrity than his mother—never to stoop to her level of betrayal. And yet he'd had to face the unwelcome realisation that his desires were no less base than his weak and adulterous mother's.

Lara watched a series of expressions flicker across Ciro's face. They gradually got darker and darker, until he was glaring at her as if she was the sum of all evil. He started moving towards her then, all coiled lethal masculinity, and Lara took an involuntary step back.

She wasn't scared of his physicality—not even with this tension in the air. She was scared of something far more ambiguous and personal deep inside where she knew he had the ability to destroy her. Where he'd already destroyed her.

He stood in front of her, his scent winding around her like invisible captive threads. He asked with lethal softness, 'Are you suggesting my life has been on hold?'

Before she could respond, a sound halfway between a sneer and a laugh came out of Ciro's mouth.

'Oh, *cara,* my life hasn't been on hold for one second since you decided to take that old man into your bed.'

Lara winced inwardly. She already knew that Ciro's life hadn't been on hold. Far from it. As much as she'd tried to block him out of her consciousness, it had been next to impossible. Since his kidnapping he'd become even more infamous and sought-after. He'd tripled his fortune, extending the wildly successful Sant'Angelo Holdings, which had been mainly focused on real estate, to encompass logistics and shipping worldwide.

And he hadn't been seen with the same woman twice—which was some feat, considering the frequency with which he'd been photographed at every ubiquitous glamorous event on the European and the worldwide circuit.

The gossip about his hectic love-life had quickly eclipsed any rumours about why his wedding to Lara hadn't taken place. Most people had assumed exactly what her uncle had wanted them to assume—that the kidnapping and fresh stories of his links to the Mafia had scared off Lara Templeton, one of Britain's most eligible society heiresses.

If anything the tone of the gossip about her had been as sneering as about Ciro—especially when she'd got married so quickly after the event, to a man more than twice her age. It was as if she'd merely proved her own snobbishness. As if she hadn't been woman enough to handle Ciro Sant'Angelo.

Certainly all the women he had been photographed with since then had run to a type that was a million miles from Lara's cool blonde, blue-eyed looks. Women with flashing dark eyes and glossy hair. With unashamedly sexy and curvaceous bodies and an effortless sensuality that Lara could never hope to embody. She was too self-conscious. Too…inexperienced.

Ciro was shaking his head now, a look of disgust twisting his features and making his scar stand out even more. 'Did you keep up the virginal act with your husband? Or did you fake it right up until—?'

'Stop it!' The sharp cry of Lara's voice surprised even herself. She felt shaky. 'That wasn't an act.'

Ciro made a rude sound, dismissing her words. More proof that she'd been utterly naive to try and defend herself. All she could hope for was that Ciro would get bored and ask her to leave.

'Look, what do you want, Ciro?' Lara's voice had a distinctly desperate tone that she didn't even try to disguise now.

'It's very simple. I want *you*, Lara.' He folded his arms across his formidable chest. 'It's time to pay your debt.'

CHAPTER TWO

LARA'S SENSE OF panic and desperation increased. 'I told—you I don't owe you anything.'

Ciro responded, 'We've been through this and, yes, you do. You owe me a wedding.'

Lara fought to stay calm. To appear unmoved. 'Don't be ridiculous. I'm not going to marry you.'

He shook his head. 'Not ridiculous at all. Very practical, actually. Like I said, I'm in need of a wife, and as you deprived me of one so memorably two years ago, you can step up now and honour the commitment you made when you agreed to marry me in the first place.'

Vainly scrabbling around for something— anything to make sense of Ciro's crazy suggestion, Lara asked, 'Why do you need a wife so badly?'

'The circles I'm moving in… Let's just say things would be better for me if I had an appearance of stability. Settling down. Conforming to societal norms of what people expect of a man my age.'

'An appearance... So this would just be a sham...a fake marriage?'

'Call it a marriage of convenience.'

'But it'll mean nothing.'

Ciro's lip curled. 'As if *that* was a concern in your first marriage... As if you *cared* about Winterborne.'

Lara had to hide her flinch at that.

Ciro continued, 'It'll be a lesson in learning that your actions have consequences.'

She took a step backwards, surprised that her legs were still working. 'This is beyond crazy. If marriage is so important to your image then I'm sure there are many more suitable women who would be happy to become your wife.'

Like any of the hundreds of women she'd seen on his arm over the past twenty-four months, for a start.

'I don't want any of them. I want *you*.'

Ciro was finding it hard to maintain his composure. Lara was right—there were plenty of women he knew who would jump at the opportunity to become his wife. He'd found himself seeking out women who were the antithesis of this woman's cool blonde looks, but none of them had made his blood run hot as she could, just by standing in front of him.

For two years his bed had been lonely and he had been frustrated. Not that the world would believe it. But he hadn't wanted any of them. He wanted Lara. And now, after two years of a kind of purgatory, hating her and wanting her, she was finally within reach again.

He would be the first to admit that his pride had suffered a huge blow when she'd walked away from him and from their marriage commitment. He was, after all, descended from a long line of proud Sicilians.

She'd accused him of only wanting to marry her to further his ambitions for social acceptance and he hadn't been able to deny it. But it hadn't been as much to the forefront of his desire to marry her as he'd let her believe. However, he had to admit that it had always been in the back of his mind…her strategic connections.

But, more than that, he hadn't been done with

her. When she'd told him she was a virgin—most likely a lie—Ciro had been stunned. To think that she was untouched…a rare novelty in his jaded world, had been, surprisingly, and seriously, erotic. The prospect that he would be her first lover had tipped Ciro over the edge of his restraint where Lara was concerned.

He'd always been traditional and Sicilian enough to envisage taking an innocent wife some day, but also cynical and experienced enough to know that it was next to impossible in this modern world. And yet there had been Lara, with her huge innocent blue eyes that had looked at him sometimes as if he was a hungry wolf, and her body with its slender lines and lush curves, telling him that she was this rare thing. An innocent in a world of cynics.

She'd led him a merry dance. Convincing him that she had something he'd never seen before in his life: an intoxicating naivety. But it had all been an act. For her own amusement. Because she'd been bored. Or as jaded as him.

Lara stood in front of him now, tall in her heels, but she'd still only reach his shoulder. For a second something inside him faltered.

Had her eyes always been so blue and so huge? She was pale now, her cheeks and lips almost bloodless. Because she was disgusted by his proposal? Good.

Ciro had to forcibly curb the urge to clamp his hands around her face, angle it up towards him and plunder that mouth until she was flushed and her mouth was throbbing with blood.

No other woman had ever had the same effect on him. Instantaneous. Elemental. He vowed right then that she would never see how easily she pushed him to the edge of his control.

He took a step back. Lara had denied him before but she wouldn't deny him now. She owed him. Owed him her body and the connections a marriage to her would bring him.

'Well, Lara?'

'This is the day of my husband's funeral... have you no sense of decency?'

Ciro could have laughed at her dogged refusal to stop acting. 'Are you telling me you really *cared* about the old man?

The thought that she might actually be grieving for her husband slid into his mind for a second before he brutally quashed it. *Impossible.*

She flushed. With guilt. Ciro didn't like the rush of relief he felt. 'Save your energy, *cara*. Your acting skills are wasted on me.'

'Stop calling me that. I'm not your *cara*.'

Her hands were balled into fists by her sides and her eyes were bright blue.

Ciro uncrossed his arms. 'You never minded it before… If I remember correctly you used to love it.' He mimicked her breathless voice, *'"Ciro, what does it mean…? Am I really your* cara*?"'*

'That was before.' Lara's cheeks had lost their colour again.

'Yes,' Ciro said harshly, angry that he noticed so much about this woman. Every little tic. 'That was when you were only too happy to court infamy by becoming engaged to me to alleviate your boredom. What I can't quite understand, though, is the virginal act? That was a touch of authenticity that deprived us both of mutual pleasure.'

It was excruciating to Lara that Ciro remembered how ardently she'd loved him. How much she'd wanted him.

Without thinking about it, just needing to

wound him as he was wounding her, she let words tumble out of her mouth. 'I never wanted you.'

As soon as she'd said the words she realised her mistake. Colour scored Ciro's cheekbones, making the scar stand out even more lividly. His eyes burned a dark brown, almost black. She was mesmerised by the fierce pride she could see in his expression. He was every inch the bristling Sicilian male now.

'Little liar,' he breathed. 'You wanted me as much as I wanted you. *More.*'

He came towards her, closing the gap. Lara's feet were frozen to the floor. He reached for her, hands wrapping around her waist, pulling her towards him, until she could feel the taut and unforgiving musculature of his body. But not even that could break her out of this dangerous stasis. She was filled with a kind of excitement she'd only ever felt with this man.

She'd thought she'd never feel it again, and something exultant was moving through her, washing aside all her reservations and the sane voices screaming at her to wake up. Pull back.

Ciro's hands tightened on her waist and his

head came down, blocking out the room, blocking out everything but *him*. Lara's breath was caught in her throat, nerves tingling as she waited for that firm mouth to touch hers. It was so torturous she made a small sound of pleading...

Ciro heard the tiny sound come from Lara's mouth. He knew this was the moment when he should pull back. He'd already proved his point. She was practically begging him to kiss her... But his body wouldn't follow the dictates of his mind. She was like a quivering flame under his hands. So achingly familiar and yet utterly new.

He could feel the press of her high firm breasts, the flare of her hips, the cradle of her pelvis. He burned for her. He'd been such a fool to believe in her innocence. He'd held back from indulging in her treacherous body. But no longer.

Ciro gave in to the wild pulsing beat of desire in his body and claimed Lara's mouth with his. For a second he couldn't move—the physical sensation of his mouth on hers was too mind-blowing. And then hunger took over. He could feel her breath, sharp and choppy, and he deepened the kiss, taking it from chaste to sexual in seconds.

Lara was wrapped in Ciro's arms, and for a moment she happily gave up any attempt to bring back reality. His touch and his kiss, that masterful way he had of touching her and bringing her alive—she'd dreamed of this so often.

His taste was heady and all-consuming. She barely noticed his hands moving up her body, cupping her face so he could angle it better and take the kiss deeper, make it even more explicit. She craved him. Pressed herself even tighter against him.

The knot at the back of her head loosened and the sensation of her hair falling around her shoulders finally broke through enough for her to falter for a moment. And a moment was all she needed to allow enough air back into her oxygen-starved brain to recall what Ciro had called her. *Little liar.* And she'd just proved him right.

She stiffened and pushed against Ciro. He let her go and stood back, but it was no comfort. Lara already ached for him. The glitter of triumph in his eyes only added salt to the wound she'd opened.

She felt totally dishevelled and unsteady on her feet. Her cheeks were hot and her mouth felt swollen. She'd just humiliated herself spectacularly.

She lifted a shaking hand to her mouth. 'You had no right to—'

'To what?' he said silkily. 'To demonstrate that our chemistry is still very much mutual and alive?'

It wasn't much of a consolation that Ciro didn't look overly thrilled about that fact.

He shook his head, his dark hair gleaming. 'In this at least you can't hide your true nature.'

He started to walk around her and Lara's skin prickled. Her pulse was still pounding. She felt raw.

'How could you do it?' he asked from close behind her. 'How could you take that man into your bed every night and let him—?'

Lara whirled around, bile rising. 'Stop it! I won't discuss my dead husband. Not on the day of his funeral. It's…immoral.'

Ciro emitted a harsh bark of laughter. '*Im-*

moral, is it? More immoral than promising yourself to a man only to leave him by the wayside as soon as you realise how close you've come to sullying the perfect Templeton family line with a brood of half-Sicilians?'

Lara's heart squeezed painfully. At one time she had fantasised about the children she would have with Ciro, wondering if they'd inherit their father's dark good looks and vital charisma. The fantasy mocked her now. She'd been so deluded.

Her voice trembling slightly, she said, 'You accuse me of being immoral, but you admitted that your motive for marriage was nothing but a cold calculation to improve your social standing.'

Ciro stood back and his dark gaze narrowed on her. She immediately felt exposed.

'There was nothing immoral about seeking out a union that would benefit us both. You really didn't have to go so far as to feign feelings for me, *cara*. It was entertaining, but unnecessary.'

Lara smarted as she recalled yet again how naive she'd been. Because it wasn't as if he'd led her on—he hadn't professed any feelings for *her*. Instead she'd pathetically read too much into every tiny gesture and word, building up a very flimsy belief that he was falling for her too.

Ciro continued. 'Why didn't you try to secure your future by giving Winterborne an heir? Is that why he left you with nothing? Because you didn't fulfil your wifely duty?'

Lara shook her head to negate what he'd said. She couldn't seem to formulate words. Memories were rushing at her in a jangled kaleidoscope of images—Ciro proposing, down on one knee in the middle of a *piazza* in Florence, with everyone looking on and clapping, the pure joy she'd felt in that moment.

And then another memory—the awful dark, dank smell of fear as she'd been jostled in the back of that van with a hood over her head. Ciro's arms had been around her and she'd clung to him with a death grip…

'I don't… I never wanted to marry—'

'Me,' Ciro interjected. 'Yes, I know.'

Lara swallowed. He'd misunderstood her. She'd wanted to marry Ciro so desperately that she was afraid if she opened her mouth now it might all spill out and then he would tear her to shreds.

She couldn't imagine—didn't want to—what he would do if he ever found out that her uncle had been behind the kidnapping in an elaborate bid to show Lara the lengths to which he would go to ensure she married someone 'suitable'.

She had to regain control of this situation and of her fraying emotions. She injected all the *froideur* she could muster into her voice. 'You've proved your point, Ciro. You haven't forgiven me for leaving you. But if it's a wife you need I suggest you look elsewhere. I'm not available.'

She turned away to leave, but before she could take a step her arm was taken by a firm hand. She stopped, every part of her body tense against the inevitable effect Ciro had on her.

He drew her back around to face him. 'Please do tell me what it is you're so busy with now that you're a free woman again?'

He dropped her arm, but the imprint of his fingers lingered. She rubbed it distractedly. She looked at him, but the truth was that she was busy with nothing, because she literally *had* nothing—as he well knew.

She had just enough money in her account to see her through a week, maybe, in an inexpensive hostel. And that was it. She had nowhere to go. No one to go to.

The stark reality of just how isolated she was hit her like a body-blow.

'The fact is you're not busy—isn't that the truth, Lara?'

It was as if Ciro was delving casually into her mind and pulling out her innermost humiliation for inspection.

She tipped up her chin. 'I'll keep myself busy finding a job, somewhere to live.'

Ciro snorted. 'A *job*? You wouldn't know a job if it jumped up and bit you. I doubt an art history degree gets you very far these days. You were bred to fulfil a role in society, Lara. Anything else is beneath you.'

Hurt hit Lara squarely in the chest. She'd once confided in Ciro about wanting to do more than what was expected of her. No doubt he thought she'd been lying.

She lashed out. 'You mean like marrying

you? We went through this once before—do you *really* want to be humiliated again, Ciro?'

This was the Lara that Ciro remembered. Showing her true haughty colours. He could recall only too easily how two years ago she'd morphed in front of his eyes into someone distant and calculating. Utterly without remorse.

It had shocked him. And yet it shouldn't have. Because it wasn't as if he hadn't already learnt how beautiful women operated at the hands of his brittle, self-absorbed mother. She'd made a fool of his father over and over again in her bid for desperate validation that she was desired.

His father had put up with it because he'd loved her, and Ciro had believed from an early age that if that was what love meant, he wanted none of its ritual humiliation.

And yet Lara had sneaked under his defences before he'd known what was happening.

His first image of her was still etched into his memory, no matter how much he'd tried to excise it. She'd been standing just a few steps from Ciro on a busy street in Florence, a hand up to her face, shading her eyes, seemingly entranced by an ornate building. She'd been like a vision of a Valkyrie princess against the ancient Florentine backdrop. Long bright blonde hair falling to the middle of her back... Acres of pale skin...

She'd been oblivious to the attention she was drawing. *Or so Ciro had believed.* But now he knew she must have been aware of exactly what she was doing, with that face of an angel and the body of a siren.

Suddenly someone had jostled her from the pavement and she'd stumbled into the busy road. She would have been hit by a car if not for Ciro grabbing her and pulling her to safety. She'd landed against him, all soft lithe curves. Silky hair under his hands. And her scent... lemon and roses. Huge shocked blue eyes had stared up into his and he'd fallen into instant lust, for the first and only time in his life. Captivated.

But memories were for fools and he would never be such a fool again. He knew who— *what*—Lara was now. He would make use of her and then discard her, exactly as she had done with him when he'd literally been at his lowest point.

'You're really not in a position to bargain, Lara. You have nowhere to go and no one to turn to. You wouldn't survive half an hour outside that door.'

Lara clenched her hands into fists. The only thing stopping her making a vociferous defence was the fact that Ciro was speaking her fears out loud. What skills did she have? What meaningful education? Where would an interesting but useless degree get her in this new digital age? Some menial job in an art gallery if she was lucky? She could probably plan and host a diplomatic function for fifty people, but in reality domestic cleaners were more highly qualified than she was.

Taking advantage of her silence, Ciro said, 'This is what I'm proposing. We will get married in Rome, exactly as we planned two years ago. I think a year of marriage should suffice, but we can review it after six months. During our marriage you will perform social duties as my faithful and loyal wife. You will open doors for me that have remained resolutely shut. And once we agree to a divorce settlement I will make you a very rich woman.'

Lara was incredulous. 'You're serious.'

'Deadly.'

He looked at his watch then, as nonchalantly as if he hadn't just made such a preposterous suggestion. 'My driver will take you back to your apartment, where you will pack up your things, and then you will return here to me. We leave for Rome this evening.'

Lara's head was spinning. Too much had happened in such a short space of time. Her husband dying. Ciro reappearing in her life. His crazy proposal, which made a mockery of his first proposal. The prospect of having to learn how to survive on her own. And now the opportunity for something else entirely.

Something ridiculous. Gargantuan. *Impossible.*

And yet all she could think of to say was, 'Why did you pretend to be a driver?'

Ciro's jaw clenched. 'Because it amused me to see you in action among your peers. Behaving true to your nature. The nature you hid from me when we first met.'

Her chest ached. The woman she'd been when she'd met Ciro—that *had* been her. Infinitely naive and innocent. But she'd learnt many harsh lessons since then, and she had to protect herself around this man or he would annihilate her.

She said, with as much coolness as she could muster, 'This conversation is over, Ciro. You've played your little stunt but I'm not interested.'

He merely lifted a brow. 'We'll see.' He extended his hand towards the door. 'My driver is ready to take you to the apartment, where he will wait for you outside.'

Without a word Lara turned and walked out. The woman who had shown her into the room was waiting with her things. Lara murmured a distracted thank you and went to the front door, where Ciro's car and driver were indeed waiting. Along with the security men.

Another shiver went down her spine as she recalled that awful moment when Ciro had gathered her in his arms to kiss her on that quiet Florentine side street and all hell had broken loose as they'd been ripped apart and then bundled into the back of a van…

She was tempted to ignore the car and walk around the corner to her apartment, but the driver was waiting with the door open and

Lara's innate sense of politeness and a wish to not cause conflict made her get into the back of the vehicle. Also, although she was probably being paranoid, she could imagine Ciro standing at a window, silently commanding her to do as he'd bade.

The journey was short and she got out again only a couple of minutes later. She noticed that Ciro's security detail hadn't followed her to her apartment. *And why would they?* she scolded herself. She was nothing to Ciro except someone he wanted to toy with for his own amusement.

And revenge, whispered a voice.

She hurried inside, needing the time alone. To her relief the apartment was empty of staff. Her few meagre belongings were packed into two suitcases, which were standing neatly in the entrance hall. A reminder to leave as quickly and quietly as possible. But Lara needed time to process everything that had just happened.

She wandered around the apartment that had been like a prison to her in the past two years. She still couldn't quite believe the sequence of events that had led her to this place: marriage to an odious man old enough to be her father.

Of course she hadn't wanted to marry him. When her uncle had suggested it she'd laughed. But then he'd revealed to her that he'd been behind the kidnapping and that he would do worse to Ciro unless she married Henry Winterborne.

Lara sat down blindly on the end of the bed for a moment, overcome with the weight of the past.

Her uncle had been in debt to the tune of millions. His entire fortune gambled away. When she'd told him defiantly she didn't need him, that she had her trust fund, which was due to come to her on her twenty-fifth birthday, he'd told her that that was gone too. He'd had access to it, in order to manage it on her behalf, and he'd gambled it away.

Even then—after his threats and after he'd revealed how far he was willing to go to stop her from marrying Ciro—Lara had still hoped that perhaps if she told Ciro he would be able to protect them. So she'd gone to the hospital where he'd been recuperating and she'd asked him if he loved her—because she'd known that if he loved her then she was willing to do anything to defy her uncle. She'd believed that once Ciro knew about the threat surely he'd be powerful enough to protect himself—and her?

But Ciro had looked at her for a long moment and hesitated. And in that moment she'd known she'd been ridiculously naive.

He must have seen her expression, because he'd said quickly, 'Love? *Cara*, I never promised you love. But I am prepared to commit to you for ever, and I respect you… Isn't that enough? It's a realistic foundation for a life together.'

He hadn't loved her. And so she'd followed the dictates of her uncle in order to protect a man she loved who didn't love her.

Lara had come back to London where she'd been introduced to Henry Winterborne and the marriage had been arranged. Her uncle had made a deal. Henry would bail him out of his debts, restore his reputation, in return for marriage to Lara. A medieval and Machiavellian arrangement.

Lara had been in a fog for days. Lost. Alone.

And all the time she was being reminded by her uncle that if she didn't comply he would hurt Ciro.

It had been on their wedding night that Lara had returned to this apartment with her new and very drunk husband and reality had finally broken through the numbing shell in which she'd encased herself.

To this day she had no real memory of the wedding, or saying her vows. It was all a blur. But on that night she'd heard her husband thrashing about the apartment, shouting at the staff to get him drinks. She'd hidden in the bedroom, telling herself that she would leave, escape…send a warning to Ciro somehow… Anything had to be better than this.

And then Henry had come into her room. Crashed through the door.

Lara had tried to get away, but he'd caught her and tried to rip her nightdress. He'd shoved her down on the bed and instinctively Lara had lifted her legs to kick him off. His bulk and his inebriated state had made him fall backwards, and he'd hit his head on the side of a dresser.

The fall and his general bad health had resulted in him being put into a wheelchair. The shock of the accident, and Lara's uncle's persistent reminders of his threats, had stopped her initial thoughts of trying to escape.

That was when she'd started to see pictures of Ciro, out and about, getting on with his life. The beautiful women on his arm didn't seem to be put off by the livid scar. It only enhanced his charismatic appeal. And seeing Ciro like that... It had broken something inside Lara. Broken any will to try and escape her situation. Any sense of optimism that perhaps she'd been wrong about him not loving her dissipated.

All hope had gone.

With the threat of physical violence from her husband negated, Lara had sunk into a routine of sorts. Days had passed into weeks, and then months, and before she'd known it a year had gone by. Henry Winterborne had got rid of his staff by then, had begun using Lara as an unpaid housekeeper and carer.

When her uncle had died, three months ago, Lara's will to leave her husband had been revived. The threat hanging over Ciro was finally gone. But without any funds of her own she'd been in no position to take legal action.

Before she'd had a chance to assess her options Henry Winterborne had had a stroke, and he'd spent the last two months of his life in hospital. For the first time in two years Lara had had a sense of autonomy again. Albeit within her gilded prison.

She caught sight of her reflection in a mirror on the wall opposite her. She took in her pale and wan features. Why on earth would a man as vital as Ciro Sant'Angelo still be remotely interested in marrying her?

An inner voice answered her: *For revenge.*

And because he had her right where he wanted her. Vulnerable and desperate. Or so he thought.

Lara might have qualms about navigating the world on her own after a lifetime of not being prepared for it, but she'd do it. She'd longed for months just to walk out of this apartment and not look back. To take her chances. But the blackmail her uncle had subjected her to and the guilt of Henry Winterborne's accident had kept her a prisoner.

And there was still guilt. Because the threat to Ciro might be gone, but it had been *her* involvement with him that had led to his kidnap in the first place. If she hadn't ever met Ciro he would never have come to her uncle's attention and would never have been put in danger.

She'd *known* that her uncle had plans for her to marry someone 'suitable'. He'd spoken of little else since she'd left school and gone to university—which he hadn't approved of at all. But Lara had never taken him seriously. It had sounded so medieval in this day and age, and at one time she'd told him so.

He'd reminded her of how much she owed him. Asked her where she would have ended up if he hadn't been there to take her in after his dear brother's tragic death. He'd reminded her of how he'd put his life on hold to make sure she was educated and looked after. He'd reminded her that his brother's death had been a devastating shock for him too, and yet he'd had no time to grieve—he'd been too busy making sure Lara was all right.

Little had she realised how deadly serious he was about marrying her off, and by the time she'd met Ciro, Thomas Templeton had been in dire straits—which had turned Lara into an invaluable commodity. And even though Ciro was a wealthy man, it hadn't been enough for Lara's uncle. He'd needed her to marry a man of *his* choosing, from the *right* side of society.

Lara willed down the nausea that threatened to rise. She needed to focus on the present. Not on the painful past.

She stood up from the bed, immediately agitated. *Ciro*. Back and looking for revenge. And could she even blame him? No. She couldn't. She'd single-handedly brought terror into his life. Forced him to live under the shadow of personal protection. Because he'd been shown to be vulnerable. Something she knew he must *hate*.

She also owed him for the resurgence in the rumours about his family's links to the Mafia, who people believed had been responsible for his kidnapping. Not to mention the humiliation of walking out on him days before they were due to be married under the spotlight of the world's media.

One of the many headlines had read *Sicilian*

Millionaire to Wed English Society Fiancée!
The article underneath had been less flattering, snidely suggesting that Ciro had been trying to marry far above his station.

The fact that Ciro had managed to ride out the storm of headlines and speculation to thrive and survive only demonstrated the scale of his ambition. But clearly that wasn't enough for him.

Her guts twisted. She'd loved him so desperately once. She would have done anything for him. And she had. Could she sacrifice herself again just to allow him to feel some measure of closure? To allow him the access he craved to a level of society that would bring him even more success and acceptance?

'A year of marriage...review it in six months.'
Ciro's cold proposal was daunting. Could she possibly even contemplate such a thing? Subject herself to Ciro's bid for revenge?

Lara stopped pacing and caught her reflection in the mirror again. Her cheeks were flushed now. Eyes over-bright.

Would it really be a sacrifice when he still

stirs up so many powerful emotions and desires? questioned a snide inner voice.

She saw the buildings and the skyline of London behind her, reflected in the mirror through the window. There was a back way out of the apartment. She knew she could leave if she wanted to. Slip away into the millions of anonymous people thronging London's streets. Get on with her life. Try to put all this behind her.

But Ciro would come after her. Just as he'd pursued her once before. Relentlessly. Seductively.

She'd kept refusing his advances at first, intimidated by his charismatic masculinity and his playboy reputation. But in the end he'd won her over, when he'd taken her to that gallery after hours.

She shook her head to dislodge the disturbing memory. All it had been was an elaborate seduction ruse. She'd been different from his other women. Naive, wide-eyed. Except now he thought it had all been an act.

Lara had already been through worse than a marriage of convenience to one of the world's most notorious playboys. Far worse. She'd lost her entire beloved family overnight. She'd been heinously betrayed and exploited by her uncle, her last remaining family member. She'd been belittled and bullied by her husband. And she'd had her heart broken already by Ciro Sant'Angelo, so she had no heart left to break.

Realising that Ciro hadn't ever loved her had made it easier for her to do what she'd had to. To be cruel. To walk away. And yet now she was contemplating walking back to him?

A voice in her head queried her sanity. After everything she'd been through at the hands of her uncle and her deceased husband she should be running a million miles from this scenario. And yet despite everything the pull she felt to go back into Ciro's orbit was strong. Too strong to resist?

Lara knew she had only one choice. She had to do what was best for her and her future, so that she could get on with her life with a clear conscience and leave her past behind once and for all.

CHAPTER THREE

CIRO FELT THE tight knot inside him ease. Disconcertingly, it was the same sensation he'd felt when one of his assistants had informed him of Henry Winterborne's death. Except that had been more acute, and quickly followed by a sense of urgency. Find Lara. Track her down. Bring her to him.

She was his now.

His driver had just rung to say that Lara had asked for help with her bags. Which meant she hadn't tried to run. She was coming back to him.

It irked him that he hadn't been sure, when he was so sure of everything else in his life. Nothing was left to chance. Not since the kidnapping.

His little finger throbbed. The missing finger. They called it phantom pain. Pain even though it wasn't there any more. A cruel irony.

He found most women boringly predictable, but Lara Templeton had never been predictable. Not even now, when she was penniless and homeless. A woman that resourceful and beautiful? He had no doubt that she could slip out of his grasp and then he would encounter her at some future event, with another man old enough to be her father.

So why had he given her the opportunity to run if she so wanted? Because a perverse part of him wanted to prove to himself how mercenary she was. She wouldn't get a better deal than the one he was offering: a marriage of convenience for a year, maximum. Minimum six months. And when they divorced she would be set for life.

He'd laid it out for her and she'd taken the bait. It was perverse to be feeling…*disappointed*. Especially when he had lived the last two years in some kind of limbo. Unable to move on. To settle.

He'd worked himself to a lather, tripling his fortune. Earning respect. But not the respect he craved. The respect of polite society. The respect of the upper echelons of Europe, who still saw him as little more than a Sicilian hustler with a dubious background. Especially after the kidnapping, which remained a mystery to this day.

His best friend, an ex–French Foreign Legionnaire who worked in security, and who had courageously rescued Ciro with a highly skilled team of mercenaries, had told Ciro that they might never find out who had orchestrated it. But one day Ciro would find out, and whoever was responsible would pay dearly.

At that moment he saw his car pull up in front of the house again. There was a bright blonde head in the back. Ciro's blood grew hot. Lara Templeton would be his. *Finally.* And when he'd had his fill of her, and had achieved what he wanted, he would walk out and leave her behind—exactly as she'd done to him in his weakest moment.

Within hours Lara was sitting on Ciro's private jet, being flown across Europe to Rome. She'd just declined a glass of champagne and now Ciro asked from across the aisle, 'Don't you feel like celebrating, darling?'

She looked at him suspiciously. He was taking a sip of his own champagne and he tipped the glass towards her in a salute. He'd changed into dark grey trousers and a black polo shirt. He looked vital and breathtakingly handsome. From this angle Lara couldn't see the scar on the right-hand side of his face—he looked perfect. But she knew that even the scar didn't mar that perfection; it only made him more compelling.

'Surprisingly enough, not really.'

She'd wanted to sound sharp but she just sounded weary. It had been a long day. She couldn't believe the funeral had been that morning; it felt like a month ago. She'd changed out of her funeral clothes into a pair of long culottes and a silk shirt which now felt ridiculously flimsy.

Ciro responded. 'Your marriage to Winterborne might have left you destitute, but fortunately you still have some currency for me. You must have displeased him very much.'

Lara had a sudden flashback to the suffocating weight of the drunken Henry Winterborne on top of her and the sheer panic that had galvanised her into heaving him off.

She swallowed down the nausea and avoided Ciro's eye. 'Something like that. Maybe I will have that champagne after all…' she said, suddenly craving anything that might soothe the ragged edges of her memory.

Ciro must have made a gesture, because the pristine-looking flight attendant was back immediately with a glass of sparkling wine for Lara. She took a sip, letting it fizz down her throat. She took another sip, and instantly felt slightly less ragged.

'Here's to us, Lara.'

Reluctantly she looked at Ciro again. He was facing her fully now, and she could see the scar. And his missing finger. And the mocking glint in his eye. He thought he was unnerving her with his scars, and he was—but not because she found them repulsive.

He was holding out his glass towards her. Lara reached out, tipping her glass against his, causing a melodic chiming sound which was incongruously happy amidst the tension.

It was a cruelly ironic echo of another time

and place. A tiny bustling restaurant in Florence where they'd toasted their engagement. Lara could recall the incredible sense of love she'd felt, and the feeling of security. For the first time in her life since her parents and her brother had died she'd felt some measure of peace again.

A sense of coming home.

The sparkle of the beautiful ring Ciro had presented her with had kept catching her eye. She'd left that ring in his hospital room when she'd walked out two years ago.

As if privy to her thoughts, Ciro reached for something in his pocket and pulled out a small velvet box. Lara's heart thudded to a stop and her hand gripped the glass of wine too tight.

Ciro shrugged. 'Seems an awful waste to buy a new ring when we can use the old one.'

A million questions collided in Lara's head at once, chief of which was, *How did he still have the ring?* She would have thought he'd thrown it away in disgust after she'd walked out.

He started to open the box, and Lara wanted to tell him to stop, but the words stuck in her throat. And there it was—revealed. The most beautiful ring in the world. A pear-shaped sapphire with two diamonds on either side in a gold setting. Classic, yet unusual.

Lara looked at Ciro. 'I don't want this ring.' She sounded too shrill.

Ciro looked at her. 'I suppose you hate the idea of recycling? Perhaps it's too small?'

'No, it's not that… It's…' She trailed off ineffectually.

It's perfect.

Lara had a flashback to Ciro telling her that the sapphire had reminded him of the colour her eyes went when he kissed her… *That* was why she didn't want it. It brought back too many bittersweet memories that she'd imbued with a romanticism that hadn't been there.

She managed to get out, 'Is this absolutely necessary?'

Oblivious to Lara's turmoil, Ciro plucked the ring out of the box and took her left hand in his, long fingers wrapping around hers as he slid the ring onto her finger, where it sat as snugly as if it had never been taken off.

'Absolutely. I've already issued a press release with the news of our re-engagement and upcoming marriage.'

There was a sharp cracking sound and Lara only realised what had happened when she felt the sting in her finger. She looked down stupidly to see blood dripping onto the cream leather seat, just as Ciro issued a curt order and the flight attendant took the broken glass carefully out of Lara's grip.

She was up on her feet and being propelled to the back of the plane and into a bathroom before she'd even registered that she'd broken her champagne glass. Ciro was crowding into the small space behind her, turning on the cold tap and holding her hand underneath.

The pain of the water hitting the place where she'd sliced herself on the glass finally made her break out of her shocked stasis. She hissed through her teeth.

'It's a clean cut—not deep.' Ciro's tone was deep and unexpectedly reassuring.

He turned her around to face him and reached for a first aid kit from the cabinet above her head, pulling out a plaster which he placed over the cut on the inside of her finger with an efficiency that might have intrigued Lara if she'd not been so distracted.

He said with a dry tone, 'While I will admit to relishing your discomfort at the prospect of marrying me, Lara, I'd prefer to keep you in one piece for the duration of our union.'

Lara's finger throbbed slightly, and just when she was going to pull her hand back he stopped her, keeping her hands in his. He was frowning, and Lara looked down. He was turning her hands over in his and suddenly she saw what he saw. She tried to pull them back but he wouldn't let her.

The glittering ring only highlighted what he was looking at: careworn hands. Hands that had been doing manual work. Not the soft lily-white hands she used to have. Short, unvarnished nails.

Suddenly he let her hands go and said curtly, 'You've been neglecting yourself. You need a manicure.'

Lara might have laughed if the space hadn't been so tiny and she hadn't been scared to move in case her body came into contact with Ciro's.

Panic rose at the thought that Ciro might kiss her. She didn't need her dignity battered again.

She scooted around him and into the relative spaciousness of the plane's bedroom, hiding her hands behind her back. She wasn't unaware of the massive bed in the centre of the room but she ignored it.

'You could have told me you were putting out a press release. This affects me too, you know.'

Ciro looked unrepentant. 'Oh, I'm aware of that. But as soon as you agreed to marry me you set in motion a chain of events which will culminate in our wedding within a week.'

'A week!' Lara wanted to sit down, but she didn't want to look remotely vulnerable. So she stayed standing.

Ciro shrugged. As if this was nothing more to him than discussing the weather. 'Why not? Why drag it out? I've got a busy schedule of events coming up and I'll need you by my side.'

Lara felt cornered and impotent. She'd walked herself into this situation after all. 'Why not, indeed.'

A knock came on the door and a voice from

outside. 'We'll be landing shortly, Signor Sant'Angelo.'

Ciro took Lara's arm in his hand, as if to guide her out, but when he didn't move she glanced at him and saw him direct an expressive look from her to the bed.

'Pity,' he said silkily. 'Next time.'

An immediate wave of heat consumed Lara at the mere thought of such a decadent thing, and she pulled her arm free and muttered a caustic, 'As if...'

All she could hear as she walked back up the plane was the dark sound of Ciro's chuckle.

Lara was very aware of the ring on her finger. She turned it absent-mindedly as she looked out of the window at the view of Rome.

She was glad they were here and not in Florence. Florence held too many memories...and nightmares.

It was where she'd met Ciro on a street one day and her world had changed for ever. He'd been in Florence to close a major deal which would convert one of the city's oldest *pala-*

zzos into an exclusive hotel. Something the Sant'Angelo name was famous for.

Not that she'd had any clue who he was at first.

She'd been pushed into the road by another tourist, blind to everything but the beauty of Florence, when someone had grabbed her and pulled her back from the oncoming cars.

She'd looked up to see who was holding her arm with such a firm grip and laid eyes on Ciro Sant'Angelo for the first time. He'd fulfilled every possible cliché of tall, dark and handsome and then some. And, even though Lara had seen plenty of tall, dark, handsome Italian men by then, it had been this one who had stopped her heart for a long second. When it had started beating again it had been to a different rhythm. Faster.

Lara had been excited and terrified in equal measure. Because no one had affected her heart in a long time. She'd locked it away after losing her family. Closed it up tight to protect herself. And yet, in that split second, on that sunny day in Florence, she'd felt it start to crack open again. Totally irrational and crazy. But it had opened and she'd never managed to close it up again.

She'd looked him up on the internet a couple of days after meeting him and absorbed the full extent of his fame and notoriety as a playboy who came from a family steeped in Sicilian Mafia history.

She'd told him that she'd looked him up. His expression had shuttered immediately, and she'd seen him drawing back into himself.

He'd said to her, 'Find anything interesting?'

She'd known instinctively that the moment was huge, and that she trusted him. So she'd said, 'I'm sorry. I just wanted to know more about you, and it was hard to resist, but I should have asked you about yourself face-to-face.'

After a long moment he'd extended a hand and said, 'Ask me now.'

She'd taken his hand and asked him about Sicily, about his business. His deep voice had washed over her and through her, binding her even tighter into the illusion that there was something real, palpable, between them.

Lara turned away from the bird's eye view of the iconic Colosseum, visible in the distance, and looked around the bedroom. When they'd arrived yesterday evening every bone in her body had been aching with fatigue. They'd eaten a light meal of pasta, prepared by Ciro's unsmiling housekeeper, and Lara had been glad that conversation had been kept to a minimum.

It had been an ironic reminder of other meals with Ciro, when they'd been happy just to be near each other. Not speaking.

That had always surprised her about him—that he didn't feel intimidated by silence. It had reminded her of when her brother would tug playfully on her hair and say, 'Earth to Lara—where are you in the world?' because she'd used to get so lost in her daydreams.

She diverted her mind away from the painful memory of her brother. And from daydreams. They were a thing of the past. A vulnerability she couldn't indulge in. She didn't believe in dreams any more. Not after losing her entire family in one fell swoop. Not after being betrayed by her uncle. And certainly not after having her heart broken into a million pieces by Ciro Sant'Angelo.

The bedroom was spacious and luxurious

without being ostentatious—much like the rest of the apartment. A pang gripped her. She knew how hard Ciro had worked for this—to show the world that he was different from the Sant'Angelos who'd used to rule and succeed through crime and brute force.

Lara sighed. She hated it that she still cared enough to notice that kind of thing.

She caught her reflection in a full-length mirror and considered herself critically, noting the puffiness under her eyes. She'd had a shower in the en suite bathroom and was dressed in slim-fitting capri pants and a T-shirt. No make-up. Totally boring. Not designed to attract the attention of a playboy like Ciro.

Surely when he saw her in the cold light of morning he'd wonder what on earth he'd done?

After pulling her hair back in a low ponytail and slipping on flat shoes, she went in search of Ciro, vaguely wondering if it had all been a dream and she'd find herself back in London.

Liar, whispered an inner voice, *you don't want it to be a dream.*

She ignored it.

But when she walked into the big living and

dining area reality was like a punch to the gut. This was no dream.

Ciro was sitting at the top of a huge table with breakfast laid out before him, reading a newspaper. His legs were stretched out and crossed at the ankle and he was looking as relaxed as if it was totally normal to have whisked your ex-fiancée off to another city straight after the funeral of her husband because you were bent on retribution.

He looked up when she approached the table and Lara immediately felt self-conscious. She wished she had some kind of armour to protect herself from that laser-like brown gaze.

He stood up and pulled out a chair to the right of his. Ever the gentleman. Lara murmured her thanks and sat down. The housekeeper appeared and poured her some coffee. Lara forced a smile and said her thanks in Italian, but the housekeeper barely acknowledged her.

'She's deaf.'

It took a second for Lara to realise that Ciro had spoken. She looked at him. 'What?'

'Sophia…my housekeeper. She's deaf. Which

is why it can sometimes feel like she's being rude when she doesn't acknowledge you.'

'Oh.'

'I'm telling you because I don't want you to upset her.'

Affronted, Lara said, 'Why would I upset her?'

'Just don't.'

It struck at Lara somewhere very vulnerable to hear Ciro defend his housekeeper. It struck her even deeper that he would think her capable of being rude to someone with a disability. But then, she'd given him that impression, hadn't she? When she'd convinced him she'd been with him purely for her own entertainment.

'You didn't have much luggage.'

Lara felt a flush working its way up her body. A burn of shame and humiliation. 'I brought what I needed.'

Ciro inclined his head. 'And I guess you're counting on me buying you an entirely new wardrobe of all the latest fashions.'

She hated the smug cynicism in his voice, but she wasn't about to explain that once her husband had become incapacited, and blamed her, she'd been reduced to being little more than unpaid help. With very little money of her own, and none from her husband, Lara had had to resort to selling her clothes and jewellery online to try and make money when she needed it.

At one point when she'd needed money for something she'd had to sell her mother's wedding dress—a beloved heirloom that she'd always hoped to wear when she married for love, and not because she was being forced into it. The fact that it was gone for ever seemed darkly apt.

Ciro took a sip of coffee. 'You'll need to look the part as my wife. I have standards to maintain.'

Lara realised that she wouldn't survive for a week, let alone months, if she didn't do something to distance herself from Ciro's caustic cynicism and bad opinion of her. She needed to develop a hard shell around her heart. He mustn't know how deeply he affected her or his revenge would be even more cruel.

She shrugged and affected a look of disdain.

'Well, you couldn't very well expect me to wear clothes two seasons out of date, could you?'

Ciro took in Lara's expression. *There she was*. The Lara who had shown her true face in his hospital room two years ago. Making him the biggest fool on the planet. And yet it didn't make him feel triumphant. Because there were those disconcerting moments when for a second she looked—

He shook his head. *This* was Lara Templeton. Spoilt and manipulative. Prepared to marry a man just because he was from the right side of society.

'I've arranged for a stylist to come and take you shopping today. You'll also be fitted for your wedding dress. I've pre-approved the design, so you don't have a choice, Lara. I want to make sure you're suitably attired for this wedding.'

Suddenly the disdain was gone. 'What will people think of me? Marrying again so soon?'

'They'll think you're a woman who has a strong sense of self-preservation. And they'll think you're a woman who knows she made a bad choice and is now rectifying the situation.'

'They'll think I'm nothing but a gold-digger.'

Ciro tensed. 'You walked out on your injured fiancé to marry a man old enough to be your father within weeks of the day our own wedding was due to take place, so don't try to pretend a sudden concern about what people think.'

Lara's cheeks whitened dramatically, but Ciro put it down to anger at the fact that he could see right through her.

He hated it that he was so aware of her with every pulse of blood through his veins. He had no control over it. It hardened his body, made him a slave to his libido.

She wasn't even trying to entice him. He wasn't used to women not preening around him. Or he hadn't been until he'd met Lara and she'd stunned him with her fresh-faced beauty.

She was fresh-faced this morning, with not a scrap of make-up, right down to the slightly puffy eyes. Something about that irritated him intensely. It was as if she was mocking him all over again. As if she knew that she didn't even have to make an effort to have an effect on him.

He gestured towards her with a hand. 'I don't

know what you're angling for with this lack of effort in your personal appearance, Lara. But after you've met with the stylist, and once we are married, I'll expect a more...*polished* result.'

Her eyes flashed bright blue at that. And then she lowered them in a parody of being demure. 'Of course.'

That irritated him even more. It was as if there was some subtext going on that he wasn't privy to.

He stood up. 'I have back-to-back meetings all day at my head office. If you need anything, this is my private secretary's number.'

He put a card down on the table in front of her. Lara picked it up. Was it his imagination or was there a slight tremor in her hand?

She still didn't look at him as she said, 'So not even your fiancée gets your personal number?'

He reached down and tipped up her face with a finger under her chin, 'Oh, some people have my personal number, Lara. The people I trust most in the world. I have a business dinner this evening, so don't wait up. The marriage will take place this Saturday, so you'll be kept busy between now and then.'

This Saturday.

Lara jerked her chin away from Ciro's finger. Even that small touch was lighting her insides on fire. Not to mention the nearness of the whipcord strength of his body, evident even though he was dressed in business attire of dark trousers and a white shirt. It was as if mere clothes couldn't contain the man.

'Worried I'll abscond?'

Ciro stepped back and put out his arm. 'You're not a prisoner, Lara. You're free to leave. But we both know that you won't—especially when you see the very generous terms of the prenuptial contract. I know the real you now. You don't need to pretend to be something else. This will be a very mutually beneficial arrangement.'

And she knew the real him. The man who wanted her only for her connections and her class. She was tempted to stand up and walk out with her head held high. Claim back her life. But she'd agreed to this because she knew what had been done to this man was her fault.

He might not have loved her, but he hadn't deserved to be treated the way she had treated him, and he certainly hadn't deserved to be kidnapped and almost killed. She had no choice but to stay. Not if she wanted to live the rest of her life with a clear conscience.

Ciro looked at his watch. 'The stylist will be here at midday and some of my legal team will come before that with the pre-nuptial contract. An assistant will set you up with a mobile and laptop—whatever you need.'

Then he was gone, striding out of the room before she could say anything.

Lara looked at the delicious array of food on the table and her stomach churned. The coffee she'd drunk sat heavily in her stomach.

The housekeeper came back just as Lara was standing up and Lara touched her arm gently. The woman looked at her questioningly and Lara smiled and said *grazie*. The woman smiled widely and nodded, and Lara felt for a second as if she'd scored some kind of tiny victory.

Ciro might think the worst of her but *she* knew who she was. She just needed to remember that.

* * *

By the time Lara had walked from the car and up the steps to the porch of the cathedral on Saturday afternoon she was shaking. There were what looked like hundreds of people lining the steps, calling out her name, and the flashes of cameras.

The wedding dress that Ciro had picked out was stunning, but far more extravagant than Lara would have ever chosen for herself. Designed to get as much attention as possible with its long train and elaborate veil. Not unlike the dress she'd worn to marry Henry Winterborne.

Her mother's dress had been simple and graceful. Whimsical and romantic. But then it had been a dress worn for love. Lara was almost glad it was gone now. Hopefully some other woman had married for love in it.

She was not unaware of the irony that for the second time in the space of a couple of weeks she was glad of a veil to hide behind.

The aisle looked about a hundred miles long from where she was standing. And she was going to walk down it alone. She wanted to turn and run. But instead she squared her shoulders, and as the wedding march began she started walking, spine straight, praying that no one would see her bouquet shaking.

The back of Ciro's neck prickled. *She was here.*

He'd heard the cacophony of shouts outside just before a hush rippled through the church. He knew she would be walking down the aisle alone—she hadn't requested any bridesmaids or attendants. She had no family. Something about that lonely image of her caught at his gut but he ignored it.

She was the type of woman who could bury one man one week and marry another a week later. She was not shy or vulnerable.

You offered her little alternative, pointed out the voice of his conscience.

Ciro ignored it. Lara might not like what people thought of her, but she'd soon forget it when she got used to the life of luxury Ciro could offer her.

He fought the desire to turn around, not liking the sense of *déjà vu* washing over him as he thought about how this day should have happened two years ago. And how it hadn't.

In the lead-up to that wedding he'd been uncharacteristically nervous. And excited. Excited at the thought of unveiling his virginal bride. Of being the first man who would touch her, make her convulse with pleasure. And at the thought of the life he would have with her—a different life from the one he'd experienced with his parents.

But she hadn't been that woman.

Suddenly Ciro felt hollow inside. And exposed. As if he was making a monumental fool of himself all over again.

The wedding march grated on his nerves. For a moment he almost felt the urge to shout out, *Stop!* But then Lara's scent reached him, that unique blend of lemon and roses he would always associate with her, and the urge drained away.

He turned to look at her and his breath caught. Even though he'd chosen the dress for its classic yet dramatic lines—a full satin skirt and a bodice which was overlaid with lace that covered her arms and chest up to her throat—he still wasn't prepared.

He'd always known Lara was beautiful, but right now she was...*exquisite*. He could just make out the line of her jaw, the soft pink lips and bright blue eyes behind the veil. Her hair was pulled back into a chignon.

His gaze travelled down over her slender curves to where she held the bouquet. There was an almost imperceptible trembling in her hands, and before he could stop himself Ciro reached out and put a hand over hers. She looked at him, and a constriction in his chest that he hadn't even been aware of eased.

Instead of the triumph he'd expected— *hoped*—to be feeling right now, the residue of those memories and emotions lingered in his gut. And relief.

It was the relief that made him take his hand off hers and face forward. The scar on his face tingled, as if to remind Ciro why they were there. What she owed him. And any sense of exposure he'd felt dissipated to be replaced by resolve.

The wedding service passed in a blur for

Lara. She wasn't even sure how she'd made it down the aisle. The mass was conducted in English, for her benefit, and she dutifully made her vows, feeling as if it was happening to someone else.

Her second wedding to a man who didn't love her. At least she'd never been deluded about Henry Winterborne's feelings for her.

Every time she looked at Ciro she wanted to look away. It was like looking directly at the sun. He was so...*vital*. He wore a dark grey morning suit with a white shirt and tie. His dark hair was gleaming and swept back from his face.

But now she had to face him, and she reluctantly lifted the veil up and over her head. There was nothing to shield her from that dark, penetrating gaze. Hundreds of people thronged the cathedral but suddenly it was just her and him.

Before, she'd imagined this moment so many times...had longed for it. Longed to feel a part of something again. A unit. A unit of love.

And now this was a parody of that longing. A farce.

Suddenly Lara felt like pulling away from Ciro, who had her hands in his. As if sensing her wish to bolt, he tightened his grip on her and tugged her towards him.

'You may kiss the bride...'

One word resounded in Lara's head. *No!*

If Ciro touched her now, when she was feeling so raw— But it was too late. He'd pulled her close, or as close as her voluminous skirts would allow, and his hands were around her face. He was holding her as tenderly as if she really meant something to him. But it was all for show.

Past and present were blurring. Meshing.

Ciro's head came closer and those eyes compelled her to stay where she was. Submit to him. At the last moment, in a tiny act of rebellion, Lara lifted her face to his. She wasn't going to submit. She was an equal partner.

Their mouths met and every muscle in Lara's body seized against the impact of that firm, hot mouth on hers. But it was useless. It was as if a hot serum was being poured into her veins, loosening her, making her pliant. Making her fold against him, letting her head fall back so he could gain deeper access to her mouth.

It was only a vague sound of throat-clearing that made them break apart, and Lara realised with a hot flush of shame just how wantonly she'd reacted. With not one cell in her body rejecting his touch. She pushed back, disgusted with herself, but Ciro caught her elbows, not allowing her to put any distance between them.

'Smile, *mia moglie*, you've just married the man you should have married two years ago.'

Lara dragged her gaze away from Ciro's and looked around. A sea of strangers' faces looked back at her, their expressions ranging from impassive to downright speculative. And there were a couple of murderous-looking beautiful women who had no doubt envisaged themselves becoming Signora Sant'Angelo.

Ciro tucked her arm into his and led her back down the aisle to a triumphant chorus of Handel's 'The Arrival of the Queen of Sheba'.

Lara somehow fixed a smile to her face as they approached the main doors, where Rome lay bathed in bright warm sunshine—a direct contrast to her swirling stormy emotions. She was Ciro Sant'Angelo's wife now, for better or worse, and the awful thing was Lara knew without a doubt that it was going to be for worse...

CHAPTER FOUR

'WELL, YOU CERTAINLY had us all fooled.'

Lara's fixed-on smile slipped slightly when she saw who was addressing her. Lazaro Sanchez. Probably Ciro's closest friend. She'd met him a few times two years ago, when he would often look at her speculatively and say, 'You're not like Ciro's other women.'

Lara had used to joke with him that he and Ciro had a warped sense of what was normal and what was not, given their astounding good-looks and success in life. Lazaro Sanchez was every bit as gorgeous as Ciro, with messy over-long dark blond hair and piercing green eyes.

Yet in spite of the Spaniard's devastating charm he'd never made her pulse trip like Ciro had. *Did.* She could still feel the imprint of his kiss from the church on her mouth and had to resist the urge to touch it.

Lara decided to ignore his barbed comment. 'Lazaro, it's nice to see you again.'

Lazaro folded his arms. His expression was not charming now. Far from it. 'I'm afraid I can't say the same. You know, two years ago, when you left Ciro in the hospital, I've never seen him so—'

'Filling my wife's head with stories like you used to?'

Lazaro scowled at Ciro, who'd interrupted them and who was now snaking a possessive arm around Lara's waist. She was intrigued to know what Lazaro had been about to say but suspected she never would now.

Then she registered what Ciro had said—*my wife*. With such ease. As if this was all entirely normal.

He turned to Lara. 'We'll be leaving shortly to take our flight to Sicily. You should go and change—there's a stylist waiting for you up-stairs.'

The manager of the exclusive Rome hotel that Ciro owned, where Lara had stayed the night before and got ready earlier, escorted her to the suite where the stylist was waiting. Lara welcomed he opportunity to get away from the hundreds of judgemental eyes. Lazaro's in particular.

In the past week, along with the wedding dress, Lara had been fitted for dozens of other outfits. Evening wear, day wear. Night clothes. Underwear. Now, as the woman and her assistant helped Lara out of the elaborate wedding dress and veil, she felt a pang of regret that this wasn't a normal wedding or marriage and never would be. She'd always fantasised about a small and intimate wedding, and the fantasy had included staying in her wedding dress all night, until her groom lovingly removed it as he took her to bed.

But she had to remind herself that she'd only ever been a means to an end for Ciro. Access into a rarefied world. So she needed to forget about fantasies of small, intimate weddings. If life had taught her anything by now it was that she was on her own and had to depend on herself.

'Bellissima, Signora Sant'Angelo.'

Lara's attention was directed back into the

room, where the stylist was standing back and looking her up and down.

The wedding dress was on its hanger again, and Lara now wore a sleeveless mid-length shirt dress in the softest blush colour. It had a high ruffled neck and was cinched in at the waist with a belt. She wore strappy high-heeled sandals. Her hair was left down, to tumble over her shoulders, and a make-up artist touched up her make-up.

For a hysterical moment she felt like an actress, about to take her cue to go on stage.

Ciro was waiting outside when she emerged. His dark gaze swept her up and down. 'You look beautiful.'

The immediate flush of warmth that bloomed inside Lara felt like a betrayal. She didn't want his words to have any effect on her. They weren't infused with emotion. They were purely an objective assessment. She was a commodity. Just as she'd always been.

He'd changed into a dark grey suit and white shirt, open at the neck. Elegantly casual. They complemented each other. He extended his arm and she took a breath before putting her arm in his, so he could lead her down the stairs to the main foyer, where people were waiting.

The crowd parted to let them through, and a few people clapped Ciro on the shoulder as they passed. Lara caught Lazaro's eye. He still had that grim expression on his face. She felt like pulling free from Ciro, so she could go over and tell him that he had it all wrong. Ciro had hurt *her*, not the other way around…

And then she glanced up and saw Ciro's scar, standing out so lividly, and fresh guilt for her responsibility in that made her keep her eyes forward until they were outside and in the back of a sleek SUV. Lazaro Sanchez was right to look at her the way he did.

'Try to smile, hmm…*cara*? You've just married the man of your dreams and you will never have to lift a finger again if you are wise with your divorce settlement when it comes.'

Lara's rattled emotions bubbled over. She turned to Ciro as the vehicle pulled into the traffic. 'I couldn't care less about the money, Ciro. You, on the other hand, are obsessed by it. I pity you—because if it all went tomorrow, what would you have?'

Stupid question, Lara.

She realised that as soon as the words were out of her mouth. He'd have the towering Sicilian pride and immense self-belief that had brought him to where he was today.

But he merely shrugged lightly and said, 'I'd start again and be even more successful.'

That stopped anything further coming out of Lara's mouth.

Ciro conducted some phone calls in Italian while they were en route, and soon they were pulling into a private part of the airport where a small silver jet was waiting.

The pilot and staff welcomed them on board and Lara accepted a glass of champagne when they were airborne. Below them Rome was bathed in a magical golden sunset.

She sneaked a look across the aisle to see Ciro holding his own glass of champagne, which didn't look at all ridiculous in his big hand. Her belly fluttered with nerves and awareness. Would he expect her to sleep with him tonight? Take it as his due? Would he force her?

She shivered. He wouldn't have to. Not like

her first husband. She diverted her mind from that bilious memory.

As if sensing her regard, Ciro turned and looked at her. She cast around for something to say—anything but what was on her mind. 'All those people at the wedding and afterwards… do you know them?'

Ciro's mouth twitched slightly. 'Of course not. They're mostly peers…business acquaintances. A small number of friends and staff whom I trust.'

Whom I trust.

Lara smarted at that. Even though he'd married her, he didn't trust *her*. She thought of the pre-nuptial agreement and how it had specified that no children were expected from the union.

They hadn't really discussed children before. Lara had just assumed Ciro would want them, as he was the last in the Sant'Angelo line.

However, for her it had been more complicated. The memory of losing her own parents and her brother had been so painful she'd always believed she couldn't have borne that kind of loss again, or inflicted it on anyone else… And yet after meeting Ciro, she'd found herself yearning to be part of a family again. He'd made her want to risk it for the first time.

Ciro was still looking at her, as if he could probe right into her brain and read her thoughts. Terrified in case he might ask her what she'd been thinking about, she scrabbled around for the first thing she could think of.

'Where are we going in Sicily?'

'My family's *palazzo*. Directly south from Palermo—on the coast.'

'Does anyone live there?'

He shook his head. 'Not since my grandfather passed away a few years ago. It was his property and he left it to me because he was afraid my mother would persuade my father to sell it or turn it into a resort. She never liked Sicily.' Ciro's jaw clenched. 'As you might have noticed from her absence at the wedding, we're not really in contact.'

Lara said nothing. He'd told her before of his mother's serial philandering, and the way his father had devoted himself to her regardless of the humiliation. How his mother had persuaded his father to move to Rome, away from his homeland of Sicily. But Ciro had spent a lot of time there with his grandfather.

Lara had always believed that his experience at the hands of his mother had explained the ease with which Ciro had believed in Lara's duplicity and betrayal. He had told her once that when he was very small she'd used to make him collude with her in hiding the evidence of her infidelity from his father. Making him an accomplice. Lara could understand how her own betrayal must have been a huge blow to his pride, and more.

But while knowing all that was very well, it didn't really do much to help her now. Ciro's beliefs were entrenched, and what she had done had merely confirmed for him that women were not to be trusted.

Lara was quiet. Unnervingly so. Ciro remembered the way she'd used to chatter when they'd first met. She'd ask him so many questions that he'd resort to kissing her to stop them. And yet there'd been those moments when no conversation had been required and she hadn't filled the silence with nonsense. She'd been just as happy not to talk. Something he'd found refreshing.

This time around he was under no illusions.

He thought of the moment just a few hours before, when he'd emerged from the cathedral with Lara on his arm. When the paparazzi's cameras had exploded into life he'd felt her flinch ever so slightly on his arm, and the sense of triumph which had been so elusive had finally oozed through his veins.

He'd envisaged that moment—the beauty marrying the beast. And yet when he'd looked down at her she hadn't had a look of revulsion on her face at being photographed with Ciro and his livid scar—she'd looked haunted by something else entirely and he hadn't liked that...

In fact, since they'd met again he'd never got a sense from her that she considered him some sort of monster—which was how he felt sometimes, when people looked at him with horror or fascination. In her eyes there was something else...something almost like...sympathy. Or guilt. Which made no sense at all.

Ciro looked over Lara's form broodingly. Her head was turned away, as if the shape of the clouds outside the window was utterly fascinating. The silk of her dress clung to her slim curves in a way that made his hands itch to uncover her inch by inch and see the bounty he had denied himself before...

He'd been such a fool. Lust had clouded his judgement the first time around. Of *course* a woman as beautiful as Lara couldn't have been a virgin. Or if she had been she wasn't one now.

No matter. Tonight she would be his in every way—wife and lover. Tonight he would slake the hunger he'd felt since the moment he'd laid eyes on her. Tonight he might finally feel some measure of peace again.

The late summer dusk was tipping into night as they made the journey up a long and winding driveway to Ciro's Sicilian *palazzo*. All Lara could see was the wide open lavender sky full of bright stars and acres and acres of land rolling down to the sea. It was quiet.

They climbed an incline, and when they reached the top she sucked in a breath.

The *palazzo* seemed to rise out of nowhere and cling to a cliff-edge in the distance; a soaring cluster of buildings with a tower that looked like something from a movie. As they got closer she could see just how massive it was. Lights shone from high windows, and they drove into a huge courtyard with a fountain in the middle. Wide steps led up to a huge open door where light spilled out. It looked incongruously welcoming in spite of the intimidating grandeur of the building.

'You said once that you spent a lot of time here growing up?' Lara said as Ciro drew the SUV to a stop at the bottom of the steps.

He cut the car's engine and put both hands on the steering wheel. Lara was conscious of the missing little finger on his right hand. It made her chest ache. She looked away.

'Yes. We were mainly in Rome, after my parents moved there, but I spent most holidays here with my grandparents. My *nonna* died when I was small, but my grandfather was alive until not long ago.'

'Were your mother's parents alive?'

His mouth compressed. 'They lived in Rome and they didn't approve of her choice of husband. They had nothing to do with me or my father—even though my father moved to Rome to keep my mother happy.'

'That was harsh.'

She'd never really realised how lonely Ciro must have been as an only child. Or how it must have looked to a young boy to see his father giving up his own heritage to keep his selfish mother happy.

Just then a young woman in jeans and a white shirt appeared at the top of the steps. Ciro saw her and uncurled his large frame from the SUV, calling out a greeting in Italian.

The young woman flew down the steps and hurled herself at Ciro, who chuckled, wrapping her in his arms. Lara's breath stopped as something very sharp pierced her heart. She hadn't seen Ciro so relaxed and easy since they'd met again. He'd been like that with her, once...

She got out of the car slowly, and as she came around to where Ciro was extricating himself from the woman's embrace Lara could see that she was a girl of about eighteen, extraordinarily pretty with long dark hair and dark eyes. She was looking up at Ciro as if he was God.

Then she saw Lara and stepped back, clapping a hand to her mouth. Her eyes were sparkling and she took her hand down, smiling so widely and infectiously that Lara couldn't help but respond.

Lara held her hand out, but the girl ignored it and embraced her warmly too. When she pulled back she said, *'Scusi...'* and then she rattled off some words in Italian that Lara had no hope of understanding.

Ciro said something and the girl stopped talking, looking embarrassed.

'Lara, I'd like you to meet Isabella. She grew up here on the estate with her family, who have cared for the *palazzo* for generations.'

Lara smiled. 'It's nice to meet you.'

Isabella smiled again. 'And you, Signora Sant'Angelo. Please excuse me. I do speak English but I forget when I am excited.'

The obvious warmth flowing between Ciro and this young woman was as unexpected as it was heartening. Lara had never seen him look so relaxed.

Isabella took Lara's arm. 'Roberto will come and get the bags—he's my twin brother. Let me show you around!'

Lara didn't think she had much choice, so she let herself be led up the steps and into the *palazzo* on a wave of Isabella's exuberance. In all honesty she was glad of a moment's respite—glad to get away from Ciro and stop overthinking everything that was to come that night.

Their wedding night.

About half an hour later Lara was led out onto an open terrace, overlooking the sea below. She could see another terrace further down, set precipitously right over the cliff. All was calm now, but she could imagine how dramatic it must be in a storm.

The rest of the *palazzo* was seriously impressive. Apparently it had undergone a major renovation in recent years, and now it was a byword for elegant sophistication and comfort.

It had an opulent cinema room, and a gym with an indoor pool. There was an outdoor pool set into its landscaped grounds. Too many bedrooms to count. Formal and informal dining rooms. A kitchen to die for. And there was even a quaint old church on the property.

Isabella had confided in Lara that Ciro was sponsoring her and her twin brother to go to university in Rome in the autumn. This was a side to Ciro that Lara hadn't seen before— philanthropic.

Isabella said now, 'I'll show you up to your suite. Ciro has asked that dinner be served here on the terrace in half an hour, but I'm sure you'd like to freshen up first?'

Lara nodded gratefully. She couldn't believe that the wedding had been earlier that same day. It felt like a lifetime ago.

She followed Isabella up the main staircase to the first floor, where the bedrooms were situated. At the end of a plushly carpeted corridor she opened a door on the right and led Lara into an exquisitely decorated bedroom suite, complete with walk-in wardrobe and en suite bathroom. There was even a balcony through a set of French doors, overlooking the sea. It was sumptuous.

Isabella left her alone and Lara slipped off the light jacket she'd been wearing over her dress and took off her shoes, sighing with relief as her bare feet sank into the carpet.

She padded over to the balcony and looked out, drawing in a lungful of fragrant warm air from the Mediterranean Sea. Dozens of different scents tickled her nostrils…lemons… bergamot? The salty air from the sea. It was paradise, and in spite of everything Lara could feel something inside her loosen and untangle.

'Surprised that the uncouth Sicilian has some taste after all?'

Lara jumped nearly a foot in the air and slapped a hand over her racing heart. Ciro was standing on a similar balcony she hadn't noticed, just a few feet away. He'd lost his jacket too, and the sleeves of his shirt were rolled up, revealing strong muscled forearms.

Lara struggled to process his words. 'No… not at all.' She was irritated that she was so skittish around him. 'I always knew you had taste. I never called you uncouth.'

Or had she?

In those awful moments two years ago in the hospital… She'd been so desperate to get out of there before he'd seen what a fraud she was…

Ciro made a noise. 'Maybe not, but as good as.'

It was impossible not to notice how right Ciro looked against the dramatic backdrop of *pala-*

zzo and cliffs and sea. As if he'd been hewn out of the very rock beneath them.

He straightened up from where he'd been leaning against the door. 'I'll take you down to dinner.'

He disappeared, and Lara was confused until she heard a door opening back in her suite and went in to see Ciro standing in an adjoining doorway. An interconnected but separate suite. She could see his bed in the background.

All at once she felt a conflicting and humiliating mixture of relief and disappointment. She knew she wasn't ready to share such an intimate space with Ciro yet. If ever. But she had expected him to want to project a united front. Ever mindful of people's opinion.

'Won't people expect us to…?'

'Be cohabiting?'

Lara shrugged, embarrassed. Maybe this was new etiquette and she was being incredibly unsophisticated to assume that all couples were like her parents, who had shared a bedroom. After all, her first experience of marriage had hardly been conventional.

'I have every intention of this being a marriage in all senses of the word, but we don't need to share a bedroom for that.'

Lara felt that like a slap in the face. Ciro would sleep with her but not *sleep* with her.

He came into the room. 'Dinner will be ready—shall we?'

Lara was about to follow him out of the room when she saw her shoes and slipped them on again, wincing slightly as they pinched after the long day. She also pulled her jacket over her shoulders, feeling a little exposed in the silk dress.

When they went out onto the terrace Lara couldn't stop an involuntary gasp of pleasure and surprise from leaving her mouth. There were candles flickering in little jars all along the wall and fairy lights strung into the leaves and branches that clung to the *palazzo*'s ancient walls.

With the moon shining on the sea in the distance and exotic scents infusing the air, it was magical. The thought that Ciro might have gone out of his way to—

'Don't get any ideas. This is all Isabella's idea. She's a romantic.'

Lara's heart sank and she berated herself. What was *wrong* with her? Throw a little candlelight on the situation and she was prepared to forget that this was a marriage of convenience built on her sense of guilt and responsibility. Built on Ciro's need for retribution.

A table had been set for two with a white tablecloth and silverware. A champagne bottle rested in a bucket of ice. Out of nowhere a handsome young man appeared to open the champagne. Ciro introduced him as Roberto, Isabella's twin brother.

Ciro lifted his glass to Lara when they were sitting down. It was a mockery against the flickering lights of all the candles. 'Here's to us, and to a short but beneficial marriage.'

Lara longed to put down her glass and make her excuses, but Isabella was back with the first course, and she looked so happy to be serving them that Lara didn't have the heart to cause a scene.

When she'd left them alone, Lara leaned forward. 'You didn't have to marry someone you despise, you know. There are plenty of women who I'm sure would have loved to be in my position.'

Ciro took a drink. 'Ah, but they weren't you, *cara*, with your unique qualities. You've been a thorn in my side for two years. I need to exorcise you to move on.'

'You mean take your revenge and in the process exploit my connections as much as possible?' She added, 'I hate to break it to you, but I don't wield half the influence my father and uncle did.'

Ciro appeared totally unperturbed by that. He flicked open his napkin. 'You wield influence just by being a Templeton. Marriage to you has automatically given me access to an inner circle that no one admits exists.'

Lara knew he was right on some level. As much as she hated to admit such hierarchical snobbishness existed. Impulsively she asked, 'Why does it matter so much to you?'

Ciro sat back, not liking his sense of claustrophobia at her question. But then he considered it. Why *shouldn't* he tell her? It wouldn't change anything. It wouldn't give anything away. It might actually show her just how determined he was to make this work. And how clinically he viewed this marriage. Even if his thrumming pulse told another story that was a lot *less* clinical.

'My father had a bad experience in England. He went to talk business with a number of potential partners. One by one they smiled to his face but refused to do business with him. He heard later that they had decided to close ranks against him. It wasn't just that he was new money—it was the rumours of where that money had come from. Had it been laundered? Did it come from the money made out of violence and crime by previous generations? He was humiliated. Angry. He made me promise to do better. To get myself a seat at the table so that the Sant'Angelo name could finally be free of negative associations.'

'Was your father the first one to try and break away?'

Ciro shook his head. 'It was his father. My grandfather desperately wanted to remove the stain of infamy from our name. He knew the world was moving on and he had ambitious plans for the Sant'Angelos. To go beyond these small shores, and Italy. He was sick of how our name engendered shock and derision. No respect. Not *real* respect. He wanted us to be accepted outside our narrow parameters. He craved the ultimate acceptance from a world that had always shunned us. But to do that we had to change our ways completely.'

Lara's eyes were wide. 'Where did he get his drive from? Presumably it would have been easier to keep things as they were?'

Ciro had been about to bring this line of conversation to an end—he'd said enough already—but some rogue urge compelled him to keep going, as if to impress upon Lara how determined he was.

'My grandfather's mother had wanted to marry a man she'd fallen in love with but he wasn't from the right family—in other words a family that the Mafia approved of. Her family threatened to kill him if she eloped with him. So, she stayed and married the man chosen for her—my great-grandfather. They had nine children and a perfectly cordial marriage, but she never forgave her family for doing that to her. She hated all the violence and oppression. She rebelled by passing on a new message to her own children—to my grandfather. A message to do things differently.'

Lara had stopped breathing. Ciro's ancestors had threatened to kill a man because they didn't sanction the relationship. History had repeated itself right here and the parallel was too cruelly ironic.

A little shakily she asked, 'What happened to the man she loved?'

Ciro waved a dismissive hand, as if it was of no importance. 'He left—emigrated to America. Does it matter?'

Lara curbed her urge to shout *Yes, of course it matters!* 'Not now, I guess, no.' She avoided Ciro's eye, not wanting him to see how this was affecting her.

'That's why it matters to me,' Ciro said. 'The Sant'Angelo name no longer has anything to do with those old and lurid tales of violence and organised crime, but the stain of infamy is still there. That kind of infamy only disappears completely with acceptance—true acceptance—in a very visible and public way. By association, you will bring a new kind of respect to the Sant'Angelo name that we've never had.'

Lara recalled how sick she'd felt when she'd seen the headlines after the kidnapping: *Mafia Heir Kidnapped and Held for Ransom... Sant'Angelo Kidnapping Proof He's Still Target for Criminals... Sant'Angelo Stocks Plummet After Kidnapping!*

She had brought that infamy into his life. And she hated to admit it but he was right, even though status meant nothing to her. She had to recognise that she'd been born into privilege—what did she know of his family's struggles to prove that they'd moved on from a violent world?

She had made the decision to do this—to make some redress for what had happened to Ciro, for what she had done. It was too late to turn back now.

He gestured to her plate. 'Eat up. Isabella's mother Rosa is a sublime cook.'

Lara saw the delicious-looking pasta starter on her plate but her appetite had fled. She forced herself to eat, not wanting to upset Isabella or her mother.

They conducted the rest of their meal in relative civility, sticking to neutral topics. When the plates for dessert had been cleared away Ciro got up with his coffee cup and went over to the wall of the terrace. Lara couldn't help drinking in his tall, powerful form. The broad shoulders and narrow hips. His easy graceful athleticism. The thought of going to bed with him…of seeing him naked…was overwhelming.

She realised she wasn't remotely prepared for such an intimate encounter with Ciro. What would he do when he discovered she was still a virgin?

A spark of panic propelled her from the chair to stand. 'I think I'll go to bed, actually. I'm quite tired.'

She winced. Her voice was too high and tight. She sounded so prim. A world away from the kind of woman who would undoubtedly be twining herself around Ciro right now, whispering seductive things in his ear.

He turned and leant back against the wall. Supremely nonchalant. He put down the coffee cup and looked at her. 'Come here, Lara.'

There was a sensual quality in his voice that impacted directly on her pulse, making it go faster. Afraid to open her mouth again, in case she sounded even more panicked, Lara reluctantly went towards Ciro. Her jacket had fallen off her shoulders and she shivered slightly in the night breeze.

'Cold?'

She rubbed her arms. 'No, I'm fine.'

I'm not fine.

Lara's hip bumped against the terrace wall. Ciro reached out and caught a strand of her hair, tugging her a little closer. The air between them grew taut. Expectant.

He looked at her hair as it slipped through his fingers, and then he said musingly, 'I don't despise you, Lara. I will admit that I felt humiliated by you for some time, but then I had to acknowledge that it was my own fault for having believed the façade you'd projected when I should have known better. No woman had ever managed to fool me before you.'

Lara's heart squeezed. It hadn't been his fault at all. 'Ciro, I didn't—'

He put a finger to her mouth. 'I don't care

about that any more. All I care about is that I've wanted you since the moment I saw you and I should never have denied myself this...'

'This' was Ciro putting his hands to Lara's waist and urging her towards him. Unsteady in her heels, and taken by surprise, Lara fell into him, landing flush against his body.

The effect was instantaneous. From the moment this man had first touched her, kissed her, two years ago, it had been like this. She cleaved to Ciro like a magnet drawn to its true north. His mouth touched hers and she gripped his shirt to stay standing. When she felt the slide of his tongue against the seam of her mouth she opened it instinctively, allowing him access.

Sicily and this place, even in such a short space of time, had touched something raw inside her. She could no more deny herself or Ciro this than she could stop breathing.

He gathered her closer and she could feel every ridge and muscle of his chest against hers, through the thin silk of her dress. And, down further, the press of his arousal against her belly. Desire pulsed between her legs. She wanted this man with a ferocity that might have scared her if she'd been thinking rationally for a moment. It was as if she was embracing the carnal to avoid thinking about anything rational.

Ciro's whole body was taut with the effort it was taking him not to swing Lara up into his arms and take her to the nearest horizontal surface, so he could lay her down and banish the demons that had been stalking him for two long years.

She felt like liquid fire in his arms. The soft contours of her body melted into his as if they'd been made especially for him. A ridiculously romantic notion that he didn't even have the wherewithal to reject right now, because he was so consumed with desire and need.

She tasted of sparkling wine and something much sweeter. And she exuded a kind of blind trust in Ciro, following and mimicking his movements. Darting out her tongue to touch his, as if she was afraid of what might happen if she was bolder. It ratcheted up his levels of arousal to a point where he had to bite back a groan. It reminded him of how she'd been before…which *had* to be his fevered imagination…

Her effect on him was as explosive as it always had been. Even though he now knew who she was and what she was capable of. It was as if that knowledge had added a darker edge to his desire. Because she was no longer an innocent—if she ever had been.

His hands couldn't rest on her waist. He had to explore her or die. Tracing over the curve of her hip, and up, he felt the silk of her dress slide over her body under his hand.

Ciro held his breath for a moment when he found and cupped her breast, felt its lush weight filling his hand, the press of her nipple against his palm. He wanted to taste her there, explore the hard nub with his tongue and teeth, make her squirm with pleasure. Make her moan…

Lara was drowning in heat and sensation. She'd never felt so many things at once. It was overwhelming, but utterly addictive. The rough stroke of Ciro's tongue on hers made her yearn to know what his tongue would feel like on her breast. He squeezed her there and her body vibrated with pleasure. It was too much. It wasn't enough.

Lara knew that she should pull back, put a

stop to this, but some vital part of her resolve was dissolving in Ciro's arms and a fatal lethargy was taking over. A strong desire to put herself in the hands of this man. To capitulate to his every command.

'I've wanted you from the moment I saw you.'

She'd wanted him too—even though it had terrified her. And two years of purgatory had only made that wanting stronger. It was one of her big regrets that Ciro had never made love to her. That she'd had no palpable memory to comfort her in the long and lonely nights of her marriage.

It was also one of the reasons she'd found that superhuman strength to push her husband off her on their wedding night. The thought of any man but Ciro touching her had been utterly repulsive.

And now she was here in Ciro's arms. And she wanted him to touch her so desperately that she blocked out all the inner voices whispering warnings.

But a tiny sliver of oxygen got to her brain and she pulled back with an effort, struggling to open her eyes and calm her thundering heart.

Ciro's eyes were so dark they were fathomless. 'Lara...'

Her tongue felt heavy in her mouth as she said, 'Is this really a good idea?'

CHAPTER FIVE

A COOL BREEZE skated over Ciro's skin and he felt a prickle of exposure. Lara looked utterly wanton with her tousled hair and flushed cheeks. Her too-big eyes. Her plump and swollen mouth.

'Yes. We are consummating this marriage. You want me, Lara. You can't deny it.'

She looked down for a moment and it incensed Ciro. He had seen the way she'd morphed into another person in front of him once before. He tipped her chin back up, expecting to see some measure of triumph or satisfaction because she knew he couldn't hide how much he wanted her, but there was nothing in those huge blue eyes except an emotion he couldn't define. An emotion that caught at his chest, making it tight.

'Say it, Lara. Admit it.'

She bit her lip and looked at him searchingly,

as if trying to find the answer to some riddle. Ciro was so used to women jumping into his arms at the slightest invitation that this was a wholly new experience.

Except it wasn't. Lara had been like this before. Hesitant. Shy. *Lying.*

'I do want you, Ciro. I always have.'

Ciro couldn't keep the bitterness from his voice when he replied. 'That was *one* thing that was honest between us at least.'

Lara didn't want to be reminded of the past. She wanted to stay in this moment. *This* moment, when she could almost pretend the previous two years hadn't happened.

A sense of urgency gripped her and she pressed against Ciro, spreading her hands on his chest. 'Please, make love to me.'

Ciro looked down at her for such a long moment that Lara instinctively started to pull back, suspecting that perhaps this was all part of his plan to humiliate her when she was at her most vulnerable, but then he made a small rough sound and grabbed her hand, entwining his fingers with hers to lead her back into the *palazzo*.

Her heart was thundering so loudly she was sure he must be able to hear it. There wasn't any sign of Isabella or Roberto and Lara was glad. This moment was too raw to be witnessed. This was no benign wedding night consummation.

Lara's hand felt tiny in Ciro's and he instinctively tightened his grip, even as he rejected the notion that she was somehow vulnerable.

Disconcertingly, it reminded him of how fragile and delicate she'd felt during the kidnapping. How he'd been afraid he'd hurt her because he was holding her so tight. But they'd ripped her out of his arms anyway, and in that moment Ciro had known—

He shut his rogue thoughts down right there. *Not now.* Never would he think of that again.

He pushed open his bedroom door and looked at Lara. She met his gaze and there was something indecipherable in her expression. Determined.

She took her hand out of his and walked into the room and over to the bed, kicking off her sandals as she went. She had her back to him and he could see her hands move. The silk dress started to loosen around her body.

She made a movement and he watched her shrug the dress from her shoulders so that it landed in a silken ripple by her feet. He was frozen to the spot, taking in the naked contours of her body covered only by the tiniest wisps of lace across her back and bottom. Nothing—no amount of anticipation—could have prepared him for this moment.

Ciro was glad she was facing away from him because he was convulsed with need and desire. Once again she was reaching inside him and turning his guts inside out—except this time he would slay the dragon, and once he'd had her she would lose the hold she'd had over him since they'd met.

Lara was practically naked, dressed only in her panties and a flimsy lace bra. She could sense Ciro behind her. Looking at her. She wasn't sure what had possessed her. A moment ago she'd been filled with a sense of bravado, but now little tremors were going through her body at the thought of facing Ciro like this.

And then she heard a rough-sounding, 'Lara...'

Swallowing her fear, she slowly turned around

and Ciro filled her vision. She could see the tension in his body, making him loom even larger than he normally did. Suddenly self-conscious, she crossed one arm over her breasts and covered herself between her legs with the other hand.

Ciro shook his head. 'No…let me see you. I've waited for this for so long.'

After a moment Lara did as he asked, dropping her hands to her sides, clenching them into fists. In the dim light of the room she couldn't see where Ciro's dark gaze touched her. But she could feel it. On her breasts, her belly, waist, thighs…between her legs.

Her skin broke into goosebumps.

Ciro walked towards her, his usual grace absent. When he stood in front of her she could see the stark expression of pure need on his face. His eyes were blazing.

'You are more beautiful than I ever imagined.'

Lara ducked her head, overwhelmed by what she saw in his eyes. 'I'm not…truly…'

He tipped up her chin and there was something else on his face now, an expression she couldn't decipher. Something like frustration.

'Yes, you are. You really don't have to put on this act, Lara. It's just us here now.'

He thought she was acting coy. She was stripped bare, save for some scraps of material. She'd never been more exposed. And he couldn't see it.

She realised she couldn't entirely blame him. After all, she'd done her best to convince him she was someone else. Someone who cared more for prestige and social standing than anything else.

'Lara.'

She looked at him and her whirling thoughts stopped. She sucked in a breath.

'I need to hear you say it again.'

Lara's heart squeezed. There was no going back. She needed this as much as he did.

She stepped closer, until they were touching and his clothes caused friction against her naked skin. She went up on her tiptoes and pressed her mouth to his neck. 'Please...' she said.

She trailed her mouth along his jaw, up to

where she could feel the rough edges of his scar on the right side of his face. He tensed, and then he put his hands on her arms, hauling her up and closer, before his mouth found hers and the whole world burst into flame.

Lara sensed Ciro shedding his clothes, but while his mouth was on hers she couldn't focus on anything except his intoxicating scent and the dark sensuality of his kiss. Deep and drugging.

When his hot bare skin met hers she stopped and drew back, dizzy from the kiss, and even dizzier when she saw that Ciro was completely naked. The breath left her body as she feasted unashamedly on his perfect form.

She'd never seen him fully naked. Broad shoulders, a wide, powerful chest with a dusting of dark hair that dissected his abdominals in a tantalising line all the way down to where his arousal jutted proudly between his legs. Her gaze stopped there, heat rising inside her at this very potent evidence of his desire for her.

'*Cara mia*…if you keep looking at me like that we won't make it to the bed.'

With difficulty, Lara raised her gaze to Ciro's again.

He took her hand and led her over to the bed. 'Lie down,' he instructed.

Lara lay down on the bed, hoping that he hadn't noticed the tremor in her limbs. Ciro stood for a long moment, his dark gaze moving up and down her body. Then he sat on the bed and lifted a hand, tracing the shape of her jaw and her mouth, which was still swollen from his kisses.

He trailed his hand down, dipping his fingers into the hollow at the base of her throat, and then over her chest to her breasts. Her nipples were two hard points, pressing against the delicate lace of her bra.

Ciro tortured her slowly, trailing his fingers between her breasts, under one and then the other, before covering one breast with his palm, its heat and weight making Lara bite her lip. She could feel the point of her nipple stabbing Ciro's palm, and instinctively she arched her back to push herself into his hand.

His mouth quirked. With an expertise that spoke of his experience he undid the front clasp of her bra and peeled the lace squares back, baring her to his gaze. He squeezed her breast gently and Lara's breath hitched. She was unprepared for the spiking of pleasure deep down in her core. Then he took his hand away and placed both hands either side of her body, so he could lower his head and…

Lara nearly jack-knifed off the bed when she felt the potent drugging sensation of Ciro's hot mouth closing over first one nipple and then the other.

He put a hand on her belly, as if to calm her. She was breathing so fast it hurt—but not nearly as much as the exquisite torture of his mouth on her flesh…the hot, wet heat, teeth tugging gently at her sensitised flesh.

Lara's whole body was on fire now, as the bed dipped and Ciro moved to lie alongside her. The hand on her belly moved down until it rested at the juncture of her legs. With the same expert economical touch he dispensed with her panties, throwing them to the floor. He touched her thigh.

'Open for me, *bella*.'

Lara opened her legs and Ciro's hand slid

down to explore where she was so aroused. It was excruciating. It was exquisite. She'd never known anything like it before.

Ciro had been a model of restraint two years before, when he'd discovered she was a virgin. So much so that she'd begun to feel seriously insecure. She'd ached with wanting him but he'd always seemed so in control.

Not any more.

Lara's nails scored her palms as Ciro massaged her throbbing flesh with his fingers before sliding one deep inside her. The sensation was electrifying. Lara instinctively reached for his wrist but he was remorseless.

'Trust me, *cara mia.*'

In the midst of this sensual onslaught Lara felt a dangerous bubble of emotion rise up. She *did* trust Ciro. Perhaps not with her heart any more, but in a very deep and fundamental way. She'd never expected to see him again, be with him again. Certainly not like this. But she'd fantasised about it in her lonely bed so many times…

Shocked and aghast at the welling of emotion—she shouldn't be feeling *emotion* right now!—she almost cried out with relief when Ciro took his hand away and replaced it with his body, settling between her legs as if it was the most natural thing in the world. As if they'd done this dance a million times before.

His weight was heavy and she revelled in it, widening her legs so that he came into closer contact with the cradle of her femininity, where every nerve-ending was pulsating with need.

Ciro had to take a breath and resist the urge to drive deep into Lara's willing body. He could feel the pulse of her desire against him, and the way she was opening like a flower under his body. He couldn't remember ever wanting a woman like this. Lovemaking for him had always held a certain amount of detachment. But here, right now, he was...*consumed*.

But then he'd always known instinctively that Lara had a different kind of hold over him. Something he hadn't encountered before. Something that made him nervous. But right now nerves were gone.

Ciro reached for and found protection, miraculously thinking of it at the last second, rolling it on with uncharacteristic clumsiness.

He positioned himself at the juncture of Lara's legs and looked down into her eyes. It was another thing he usually avoided with lovers, but with Lara he couldn't seem to move unless his gaze was locked onto hers.

Her expression was soft, unfocused. Her cheeks were flushed. Damp strands of her hair clung to her forehead. She was biting her lip.

'Ciro...please.'

In this there was no *other Lara*. He had undone her, exposed her.

He felt her move beneath him and couldn't hold on. He plunged deep inside her, feeling every muscle in his body spasming with pleasure at the sheer sensation of his body moving deep into the clasp of hers.

The very *tight* clasp...

It took a second for him to register in his overheated brain that Lara had tensed, and now she looked anything but unfocused. There was an expression of shock on her face. Awe. And... *pain*?

Ciro moved slightly and she sucked in a breath. His brain didn't seem to be working properly. He knew he was big but he'd thought she'd be experienced enough...

'Lara, am I hurting you?'

'It's okay...don't stop now. Please don't stop.' She sounded breathless.

She put her hands on his hips, and even as a very uncomfortable truth made itself graphically known to him Ciro could no more deny his primal urge to move than he could stop breathing.

Lara consciously relaxed her muscles, and for a second she almost cried out because the sensation was so intense. But as Ciro started to move again she could feel the pain easing, her body adapting to his, softening around him. And then, pleasure became the dominant sensation as the steady, rhythmic glide of Ciro's body in and out of hers led to a rising excitement, a sense of urgency and desperation that made her reach around to clasp his firm muscular buttocks, silently pleading with him to go deeper, faster...

Lara wasn't prepared for the sudden rush of intense pleasure. It was so unexpected and overwhelming that it was all she could do to cling on to Ciro as his body bucked into hers, again and again, as he too was torn apart and lost all control, finally slumping against her, his head buried in her neck, his ragged breath warm against her damp skin.

For those few moments while they were still intimately joined, their pulses racing, Lara knew complete contentment. Something she hadn't experienced in a very long time. But then Ciro moved, and she winced slightly as he extricated himself from her embrace. Her muscles were tender.

Ciro wasn't looking at her. He sat on the edge of the bed, his back to her, head downbent. His breathing was still uneven. Lara felt a chill skate across her bare flesh and instinctively reached for a sheet to cover herself.

After a moment he got up without a word and went into the bathroom. Lara heard the hiss of the shower. She lay in bed with the sheet pulled up over her chest, totally unsure of herself and not knowing how to behave.

Should she join Ciro in the shower? It seemed like the kind of thing a sophisticated lover would do… But he hadn't said anything and perhaps he wanted to be alone.

He suddenly emerged from the bathroom, taking Lara by surprise. He had a towel slung around his waist and his skin glistened with moisture. For a second she was breathless at the mere thought that moments ago they'd been joined as intimately as it was possible to be joined with another person.

He said, 'I've run you a bath. You'll be sore. Then we need to talk.'

Lara swallowed. Had it been that obvious? Had he noticed she was—*had been*—a virgin?

Feeling totally exposed, and far too vulnerable after what had just happened, Lara got up from the bed as elegantly as she could and went into the bathroom, trailing the sheet behind her.

After the bath, which soothed her tender muscles and her skin, Lara got out and dried herself perfunctorily. She pulled on the voluminous terrycloth robe hanging on the back of the door and steeled herself before going into the bedroom.

But it was empty.

She went out through the door and took a deep, shaky breath before going in search of her husband.

Lara had been a virgin. Innocent. Untouched.

Ciro was feeling such a conflicting mass of emotions and sensations that he couldn't quite pin down what was most prominent: anger, confusion...or, worst of all, a humiliating level of relief at knowing that *he* had been Lara's first lover and not that old man.

With that relief came more confusion and anger, and in the midst of it all was a residual heavy feeling of sexual satisfaction on a level he'd never experienced.

Before, it had been a fleeting thing. Soon forgotten. Much like the women he'd slept with, *before*. But this satisfaction felt as if it was seared into his bones and as his hunger grew for her again. Already. Insatiably.

There had been a moment out on the terrace, after Lara had said, *'Please make love to me...'* when for a split second Ciro had been tempted to reject her. As she'd rejected him. And yet even though he might have fantasised about such a moment in the previous two years, when it had been there, right in front of him, he'd been aware of how petty it was.

And also that he didn't have the strength to reject her. Not when his mouth had been full of her taste and his hands imprinted with the shape of her body.

Madre di Dio.

He heard a noise at that moment.

Lara.

Ciro's whole body tensed against the inevitable reaction his new bride would precipitate. His new *virgin* bride.

Lara tracked Ciro down to a room she hadn't yet been in. A state-of-the-art modern study with humming computers and shelves full of books and periodicals.

He was standing at a window which looked out over the sea. He'd dressed in low-slung faded jeans and a T-shirt. Bare feet. Messy damp hair. She could see his face reflected in the window. The long white line of his scar. His hands were shoved deep in his pockets, which pulled the material of his jeans taut across the perfect globes of his bottom.

Her heart thumped. 'Ciro…look…'

He turned around and she saw the full extent of his anger on his face. '*Dio,* Lara. How the *hell* were you still a virgin?'

'How did you know?'

Even as she asked the question she wanted to kick herself for being so stupid. A man as experienced as Ciro? Of *course* he'd known. He wasn't some boorish bully like her first husband had been.

He emitted a harsh-sounding laugh. 'How did I *know*? I felt it in your body and there was blood on the sheets.'

A hot wash of humiliation rushed up under Lara's skin. She hadn't even noticed the blood. She felt utterly gauche. She pulled the robe around her, tightening it.

Ciro sent her a dark look. 'It's a bit late for that.'

Lara noticed a drinks cabinet in the corner of the room. 'Can I have a drink, please?' She needed something if this was going to be the tone of their conversation.

Ciro went over and asked tightly, 'Brandy?'

Lara shook her head. 'No—anything but that.'

He poured something into a glass, then came and handed it to her. 'It's whisky. What do you have against brandy?'

Lara took the glass, relieved that Ciro was distracted from his inevitable questions for a moment. 'Brandy reminds me of funerals. When my parents and brother died my uncle made me drink some. He said it was for the shock but it made me sick.'

She took a sip of the whisky, wincing at the tart, acrid taste. It slid down her throat and landed in her stomach, sending out a glow of warmth. But she knew it was just illusory and wouldn't last.

'How old were you?'

Lara glanced at Ciro warily. 'Thirteen.'

'You were close as a family?'

Lara nodded, her hand clasping the glass. 'The closest. My parents loved each other and they loved me and Alex. We were a very happy family.'

Ciro surprised her by saying, 'You were lucky

to have had that, even if only for a short while. My father loved my mother, but it was a suffocating love and she wasn't happy to be adored by just one man. After he died she remarried within a month. She's now on husband number three—or four. I've lost count.'

The careless tone in Ciro's voice didn't fool Lara. He couldn't be immune to the fact that his mother had failed to be the kind of mother every child deserved. No wonder he was so cynical.

Ciro sat back against his desk, and folded his arms. The reprieve was over. 'So. Are you going to explain to me how you were married but still a virgin?'

Lara took another fortifying sip of whisky and sat down on a chair behind her. Her legs didn't feel steady all of a sudden. She looked up at Ciro and then away. She didn't want to see his expression.

'On our wedding night Henry came into my bedroom expecting to—' She stopped.

'Go on.'

Lara felt sick. She looked at him. 'Do we really have to discuss this now?'

Ciro nodded. Grim.

He stood up and pulled over a chair so that he was opposite Lara, sat down. She knew he wouldn't budge until she'd told him the ugly truth.

'On our wedding night he came into my bedroom… He…we'd agreed that we wouldn't share a room. I somehow…obviously naively… assumed that would mean he wouldn't try to…' She faltered and stopped.

'Try to…*what*? Sleep with his new *wife*? A natural expectation, I would have thought.'

Lara hated Ciro's faintly scathing tone. It scraped along all the raw edges of the memories crowding her head. She stood up and went over to where he'd been standing, at the window. She could see dark clouds massing over the sea and the white edges of rough waves. There was a storm approaching.

It was easier to talk when Ciro wasn't looking at her. 'He came into the bedroom. He'd been drinking all day so he was very drunk. He grabbed my nightdress and ripped it. Before I could stop him he'd pushed me backwards onto the bed. I was in shock… I couldn't move for a moment… He was so heavy and I couldn't breathe…'

Lara didn't even hear Ciro move. He caught her arm and turned her around to face him. She'd never seen that expression on his face before—disgust mixed with pure anger.

'He tried to rape you?'

Lara nodded. 'I thought we had an agreement…that he was just marrying me for appearances. He was old… I didn't think…' She trailed off, humiliated by her naivety all over again.

Ciro was grim. 'Old men's libidos can be voracious.' Then he shook his head. 'Did you really think he wouldn't demand sex from you?'

Lara pulled her arm free and moved away. Some liquid slopped out of her glass and she looked at the carpet in dismay.

'Leave it—it's nothing.'

Ciro took the glass and put it down. Lara flinched minutely at the clatter against the silver tray.

'But he didn't rape you?'

Lara looked at Ciro, remembering how thinking of him had given her the strength to deal with Henry Winterborne. 'No. I managed to kick him off me…somehow. He was unsteady from the drink. He fell backwards. He injured himself badly in the fall…and he was in a wheelchair for the rest of our marriage. Eventually he had a stroke—that's how he died.'

Lara couldn't excise the memory of Henry Winterborne's bitter words from her head. *'You little bitch—you'll pay for this. Your only currency is your beauty and innocence. Why the hell do you think I paid so much for you?'*

Fresh humiliation washed over her in a sickening wave. She hadn't even known until then the full extent of her uncle's machinations—that he'd actually sold her like a slave girl. Ciro didn't know the half of it.

Ciro was reeling. All he could see in his mind's eye was that paunchy old man shoving Lara down onto a bed and then climbing on top of her like a rutting bull. Anger bubbled in his blood. No, worse—a ferocious fury that she had put herself in harm's way like that.

'Was the prospect of marrying me really so repulsive that you would choose a man capable of rape over me? *Dio,* Lara…'

He turned around and speared a hand through his hair, not wanting her to see the emotions he couldn't control. He'd thought he'd underestimated her before. This put a whole new perspective on her ambition.

She stayed silent. Not responding.

Ciro steeled himself before turning. Wild dishevelled blonde hair trailed over her shoulders. The robe had fallen apart slightly, to reveal the plump globes of her high firm breasts. Breasts he could still feel in his hands and on his tongue...

Her eyes were huge and he hated her ability still to look so...*innocent*. Even when he'd just taken that innocence in a conflagration that had left him feeling hollowed out and yet hungry for more.

He felt the need to push her away. Gain some distance. He couldn't think when she was so close. When she was telling him things...putting images into his mind that made him want to go out and put a fist through the face of a man who was already dead.

Her silence grated on his nerves. It was as if there was something she was withholding.

'Was it that important to you? Status?'

Her eyes flashed. 'You have some nerve when you've admitted you only wanted to marry me for one thing—my connections.'

Ciro's gut was a mass of tangled emotions he really didn't want to investigate. But this woman had always touched more than just his body. A minute ago he'd wanted to put push her away and now he needed to touch her. *Damn her.*

He closed the distance between them, noting with satisfaction how a line of pink scored each of her cheeks. She couldn't hide her reaction. It was the only honest thing between them.

He slid a hand around the back of her neck, felt the silky fall of her hair brushing his hand. 'Not just for your connections, *cara mia*, but also because I wanted *you*. Your social connections and impeccable breeding were a bonus.'

Ciro's words dropped like the poisoned barbs they were into Lara's heart. And yet could she blame him when she'd convinced him that she'd never intended to marry him?

She pulled away, hating the way her body was reacting to his proximity. Excitement was building already, heat melting her core. She was still so sensitised she was afraid that if he even kissed her it would be enough to send her over the edge.

'Well, you've had me now. I'm sure the novelty is already waning.'

Ciro easily closed the distance between them again, and this time he took Lara's elbows in his hands, tugging her towards him. All she could see was that wicked sculpted mouth, and all she could think about was how it had felt on her body. Against her skin.

'Waning? I've wanted you since the moment I laid eyes on you, *cara*, and you've haunted me for two years. Believe me, once is nowhere near enough to sate my appetite.'

His mouth was on hers and Lara couldn't formulate another word. All she knew was that for a while at least there would be no more cruel words. Her heart was pounding, blood flowing to every tender part of her...

Ciro swung Lara up into his arms as if she weighed no more than a bag of flour. She knew she should protest, try to reclaim some minute modicum of dignity, but as he carried her back upstairs she couldn't help but think of how she'd endured two barren years of regretting the fact that she hadn't slept with Ciro.

So she wasn't going to regret a single moment now. No matter how much Ciro might resent her for this inconvenient desire he felt. It would burn out, sooner or later, and this time, when Lara walked away, she would have no regrets.

When Lara woke the following morning she was in her own bed. Naked. The French doors were open and the white drapes were moving gently in a warm breeze. She grabbed for a sheet, pulling it up over her chest even though she was alone.

She had a very vague memory of Ciro carrying her into this room as dawn had been breaking over the horizon, the storm clouds of the previous night banished.

Silly to feel bereft when he'd told her he didn't think it necessary for them to share a room. After all, he wasn't interested in morning-after intimacy. In a way, Lara should be grateful that this time around all the romantic illusions she'd harboured were well and truly shattered.

She tried to absorb everything that had happened in the space of twenty-four hours but it was overwhelming. This time yesterday she'd still been a single woman, on her way to get married.

She'd still been a virgin.

And now...she felt transformed.

She didn't want to admit that Ciro's touch had had some kind of mystical effect on her—but it was true. In spite of the way he felt about her, his touch had soothed something inside her— the lonely place she'd retreated to for the past two years in a bid to survive an impossible situation.

She heard a familiar low rumble and got out of bed to investigate, pulling on a robe as she did so. She went over to the French doors that led out to the balcony, knotting the robe around her.

Hesitantly she peeked over the railings, to see Ciro standing on the terrace below. He was dressed in those faded jeans and another T-shirt and Lara's mouth dried. He reminded her too painfully of when they'd first met in Florence and he'd been casually dressed. When she'd fallen in love with him.

At that moment Ciro turned around and looked up. Lara stepped back hastily, her heart spasming. *Love.* Did she still *love* him?

No. The rejection of such a disturbing thought was swift and brutal.

How could she still love a man who had betrayed her as much as he believed she'd betrayed him? After years of protecting herself from the pain of loss Ciro had come along and smashed aside her petty defences. Leaving her vulnerable all over again. She'd never forgive him for that.

Enduring all the things she had, had made her strong. Strong enough to withstand this marriage so she could finally move on with her life, her conscience salved. But the little whispers of that conscience told her that as much as she might try to justify why she was doing this, she wouldn't be here unless deeper motives were involved. Far more personal motives.

After all, if she'd really wanted to she could have told Ciro the full truth from the start. Or even last night, when she'd had a chance. But she hadn't. *Why?*

She knew the answer. Because however much he disliked her now—resented her, even, for this desire that burned between them—he would truly despise her if he knew about her uncle and his involvement in the kidnapping and ruination of their wedding. In the very public humiliation Ciro had gone through.

Lara knew that after eroding Ciro's trust in her so effectively he would never believe she hadn't had a part in it… She also knew it would be another huge blow to his pride to find out that she'd known who was behind the attack. He'd never forgive her for that.

There was a peremptory knock at her door and Lara whirled around, expecting to see Isabella. But it was Ciro. Immediately her belly clenched at the memory of how he'd felt between her legs, surging into her body over and over again.

'Buon giorno, mia moglie.'

There was something so palpably satisfied about his tone that Lara injected as much coolness into her voice as she could when she answered. 'Good morning.'

'I've decided that we're leaving today. We've been invited to an event in London tonight.'

Feeling prickly at how cool he appeared to be after a night in which her world had been seismically altered, she said, 'You mean *you've* been invited.'

Ciro leant against the doorframe and folded his arms. 'No, *we've* been invited. To the Royal Opening of the Summer Exhibition at the Longleat Gallery.'

Lara was impressed. Henry Winterborne had been incandescent with rage last year when he hadn't received an invitation to the opening. He'd blamed *her*, of course.

Ciro straightened up. 'Isabella is on her way up with a breakfast tray. We'll leave in an hour. I've arranged for a stylist to deliver some clothes to the townhouse in London, so you don't need to pack.'

He walked away and Lara breathed out slowly, her pounding pulse mocking her attempts to affect the same coolness as Ciro exuded so effortlessly. But then what had she expected? Morning-after cuddles and tender enquires as to how she might be feeling?

Lara turned around to the view again. She would be sorry to leave Sicily so soon, but at the same time she was a little relieved. It had been a cataclysmic twenty-four hours and it would surely be easier to deal with Ciro and try to maintain some emotional distance from him in a busy city surrounded by people, than here, in this effortlessly seductive and intimate environment.

CHAPTER SIX

CIRO WAS AWARE that he should be feeling more satisfied than he was. And that irritated the hell out of him.

Lara was standing a few feet away, a vision in a long yellow evening dress. She effortlessly stood out from the crowd. The dress was one-shouldered, revealing the alluring curve of her bare shoulder and the top of her back. A decorative jewel held the dress over her other shoulder. All it needed was a flick of his fingers and it would be undone, letting the dress fall down to expose her beautiful breasts—

Basta! Ciro cursed his overheated imagination.

Her hair was smoothed back and tied low at the nape of her neck in a loose bun. Long diamond earrings glittered from her ears. She wore minimal make-up. She epitomised cool elegance, and yet all he could think about was the fire that lay under her pale skin. The ardent passion with which she'd made love to him last night. It was hard to believe she'd been a novice...but she *had* been. And that bugged him like a thorn under his skin.

How had he missed it? He who considered himself a connoisseur of women?

He didn't like getting things wrong. Underestimating people. He'd learnt a harsh and brutal lesson at the hands of those kidnappers. The kidnappers who'd yet to be caught and whom he was still investigating—with not much luck.

Until that day he would have been the first to admit that life had always come easily to him. Blessed with good looks, a keen intellect and a sizeable family fortune, he'd lacked for nothing. But since those days at the hands of violent thugs Ciro had learnt not to be so complacent. And since the day Lara had informed him she'd never had any intention of marrying him he'd learnt not to underestimate anyone.

His cynicism had become even more pronounced. Any kind of easy charm he'd displayed before had become something much darker.

Unbidden, a memory resurfaced at that moment. Lara, not long after they'd met, admitting to him sheepishly that she'd looked him up on the internet. He'd immediately felt betrayed. And disappointed. She was like everyone else. Assessing his worth. Looking for the salacious details of his family history.

And then she'd stunned him with an apparently sincere apology, saying that she should have asked him face to face. Normally he abhorred women trying to get him to reveal personal details, but within seconds he'd been saying to Lara, 'Ask me now.'

That was the night she'd confided in him about her family and their history. How she had a trust fund worth millions. For the first time in his life someone had surprised Ciro. And it had only added to her allure.

Until she'd pulled the rug out from under his feet.

For the first time in a long time he wanted to know *why* she'd done it. Created that persona. But something held him back. Some sense of self-preservation. A feeling that he'd be exposing himself if he asked the question.

As if sensing his brooding regard, she turned and looked at him, and for a second Ciro couldn't breathe. She was so beautiful. And the memory was so vivid. He could almost imagine that the previous two years hadn't happened.

But they had.

He cast aside memories and nebulous dangerous thoughts. She was here by his side. *His.* That was all that was important.

He lifted his hand and crooked a finger, silently commanding her to come to him. He saw the way her eyes flashed, the subtle tensing of her shoulders. The resistance to his decree. But then she came. Because she was here in her own milieu and of course she wouldn't cause a scene.

It was time to remember why he had spent two years keeping tabs on her and why he'd married her at the first opportunity. For revenge, yes, but so much more. He caught Lara's hand in his, very aware of the absence of his little finger. The reminder firmed his resolve to stop thinking of the past.

He bent his head close to hers, inhaled her scent drifting up to tantalise his nostrils and threatening to dissolve that resolve. He directed Lara to look across the lawn to where heads of state, royalty and A-list celebrities sipped champagne and mingled. 'Do you see Lord Andrew Montlake over there?'

Lara nodded.

'He was a friend of your father's, yes?'

Lara nodded again. 'Yes—a good friend.'

Ciro smiled. 'Good, then introduce me. I've been trying to get a meeting with him for months, to discuss the chateau he's selling outside Paris.'

A few hours later Lara's feet were aching almost as much as her facial muscles ached from smiling and pretending that it was totally normal to be back in London society with a new husband just over a week after burying her previous husband. She'd felt every searing look and heard every not so discreet whisper and had held her head high with a smile fixed in place.

They were in the back of Ciro's car now, and she looked out of the window at the streets of London bathed in late summer sunshine. Young couples stood hand in hand outside pubs, drinking and laughing. Carefree.

She'd never had the chance for a life like that. As soon as her uncle had taken over his role as guardian he'd had his nefarious plan mapped out for Lara and she'd been totally unaware of it.

Pushing down the uncharacteristic welling of self-pity, Lara thought of the event they'd just been to. As much as *she'd* been the centre of attention, so had Ciro. Lara had noticed the looks and whispers directed his way too, the way people's eyes had widened on his scarred features. It had made her want to stand in front of him and stare them down. Shame them for their morbid fascination.

She'd seen the masterful way he'd operated, winning people around, charming them into submission. He might have needed someone like her for access into this rarefied world, but it wouldn't be long before he became an indelible part of it. And then her role would be obsolete.

Ciro turned to look at her then, as if aware of her regard. The back of the luxury car suddenly felt tiny. All evening Lara had been acutely aware of Ciro, of his every movement as he'd taken her hand, or touched her arm, or the small of her back. Her skin felt tight and sensitive. Her body ached with a wholly new kind of yearning. And her lower body tightened with need every time his dark gaze rested on her. Like now.

She didn't feel in control of herself at all any more. If she ever had around this man. And she hated it that he seemed so cool, calm and collected.

If he so much as touched her right now she knew she wouldn't be able to control her re-action, but he surprised her by saying, 'We're going to stay in London for a few days. I have some meetings lined up.'

Lara hid her skittishness and said, 'Fine.'

And then, just when she thought she could gather herself, he reached for her, taking her hand and tugging her across the divide in the seat, closer to him.

'What are you doing?' Lara cast a glance at the driver in front.

Ciro said something in Italian and the pri-vacy window went up, cocooning them in the back of the blacked-out car. The streets outside faded into insignificance as Ciro's hand sneaked around the back of Lara's neck, where with deft fingers he loosened her hair so it tumbled over her shoulders.

Lara's heart rate increased as Ciro's fingers massaged her neck—and then his hand moved to where the dress was held up by the jewel over one shoulder.

Excitement curled low in her abdomen as she protested weakly, 'Ciro…we're in the back of the car…'

He said, 'Do you know how hard it's been for me to keep my hands off you all evening?'

She shook her head, mesmerised by the look on his face. She could see it now—the desire bubbling just under the surface, barely restrained—and she felt it reach out and touch her.

With a flick of his fingers the dress opened and loosened around her breasts. She gasped and put a hand up, but Ciro caught her hand and said roughly, 'Leave it.'

Ciro peeled her dress down, uncovering her breasts. Lara shivered with a mixture of arousal and illicit excitement, aware of the people out-side the car on the pavement, where they were stopped at some lights. Only the blacked-out windows and some steel and glass separated her from them and their eyes.

Ciro looked at her and cupped her naked breasts, thumbs moving back and forth over her nipples. 'So beautiful,' he breathed.

'Ciro…' Lara was almost panting. She stopped talking, afraid of exposing herself even more.

His dark head bent towards her, and when his mouth closed around one tight tingling nipple the spiking pleasure was so intense she speared her hands in his hair. She quickly got lost in the maelstrom Ciro had unleashed in her body, knowing that she was showing her weakness but unable to do anything about it…

Ciro looked at himself in the mirror of his bath-room and took in his glittering eyes and the still hectic colour on his cheekbones. When they'd returned to the townhouse a short while before Lara had all but fled up the stairs, holding up the top of her dress with one hand, her hair in a tangle.

Ciro had let her go, even though he'd wanted to carry her straight to his bedroom and to his bed. The only thing that had stopped him was the awful suspicion that he'd just exposed himself spectacularly.

Just an hour before he'd been talking with one of Europe's heads of state, and within minutes of getting into a car with Lara he'd been all over her like a hormone-fuelled teenager.

He splashed cold water on his face, as if that might dilute the heat raging in his body. After a moment he went into his bedroom, restless and edgy. He looked at the interconnecting door between his and Lara's rooms for a long moment before going over and opening it quietly.

She was in bed. Curled up on one side in a curiously childlike pose, her hair spread out on the pillow. Her breaths were deep and even.

Something about the fact that she could find the equilibrium of sleep so easily made him feel even more exposed.

He went back into his bedroom and closed the door. And then he did the only thing he could do to try and dilute the sexual frustration in his body. He headed for the gym.

* * *

As soon as Lara was sure that Ciro had left her room she turned on her back and sucked in a deep, shuddering breath. She looked up at the ceiling.

She was in her underwear under the covers. She'd heard Ciro moving about next door, and after coming so spectacularly undone in the back of his car had felt far too raw to be able to deal with seeing him again. So she'd dived under the covers and feigned sleep even as her body had mocked her, aching for Ciro's touch. For him to finish what he'd started.

This evening had been a salutary lesson in the reality of how this marriage would work. Ciro had used her with a ruthless and clinical precision to seek out meetings with the various people he was interested in talking to. She had to remember that was the focal point of the marriage—her desire to make amends to Ciro for what her uncle had done to him.

What she *had done to him.*

And the other stuff? The physical chemistry? The aching desire he'd awoken in her body?

A man of his extensive experience would

surely lose interest soon. Wouldn't he? And when he did she'd have to live with that. She'd lived with far worse, so she would cope. She'd have to.

The following days brought a reprieve of sorts for Lara. Ciro was out at meetings all day, and each evening he had a business dinner to attend, where she wasn't required.

Like a coward, she'd taken the opportunity to make sure she was in bed by the time Ciro came home, pretending to be asleep if he came into her room.

She'd got used to her surroundings—just a stone's throw from the old apartment she'd shared with Henry Winterborne—but she deliberately made sure to avoid that street if she was out of the house, and she knew the security men must think she was mad, taking such a long way round to go to the shops.

Ciro had issued her with a credit card, and Lara had swallowed her pride and taken it. After two years of feeling trapped, due to her lack of personal finances, she was embarrassed at being beholden to someone else. More than ever she wanted to make her own money. Be independent.

And yet there was something about Ciro handing her some economic freedom that made her feel emotional. A man who had a lot less reason to trust her than her previous husband was trusting her with this.

She'd also got to know the staff who worked in the house: the housekeeper was called Dominique, and there was a groundsman/handyman called Nigel. Dominique hired in staff as and when it was required for entertaining or cleaning, she'd told Lara. But as yet Ciro hadn't actually ever entertained in the house.

Fleetingly Lara wondered again at the coincidence that had Ciro's new house right around the corner from where she'd been living.

One evening it was Dominique's night off— she lived close by, so didn't stay over at the townhouse—and Lara went into the kitchen, feeling restless.

She'd always loved to cook, so when Henry Winterborne had maliciously turned her from wife into housekeeper she'd welcomed it, far preferring to be in the kitchen than to share space in his presence.

She'd learnt to cook in the first instance from her parents' housekeeper—a lovely warm woman called Margaret, who had been more like a member of the family than staff. And then over the years she'd continued to cook... usually surreptitiously, because her uncle hadn't approved of her doing such a menial thing.

'You were not born to cook and serve, Lara,' he'd said sharply.

No, she thought bitterly, she'd been born so he could exploit her for his own ends.

She shook her head to get rid of the memory and looked around the gleaming kitchen, instinctively pulling out ingredients from the well-stocked cupboards and shelves.

As she cooked from memory she felt a peace she hadn't experienced in weeks descend over her. She tuned the radio to a pop station and hummed along tunelessly.

In a brief moment of optimism she thought that if things continued as they were going, and if she could maintain her distance from Ciro, she might actually survive this marriage...

* * *

Ciro had returned home early, to change for a dinner event. He was irritable and frustrated—which had a lot to do with the workload he'd taken on and the fact that he'd barely seen Lara since that first night in London.

Somehow she was always conveniently in bed when he got home, and he was not about to reveal how much he wanted her by waking her up like some kind of rabid animal to demand his conjugal rights.

He wasn't sure what he'd expected to see on his arrival this afternoon, but it involved an image along the lines of Lara being ready and waiting for him to take her to his bed when he got in.

He set down his briefcase in the hall and loosened his tie. For the first time in his life a woman wasn't throwing herself at Ciro.

He scowled. *The second time in his life.*

The first time had also been with Lara. She'd been like a skittish foal around him when they'd first met. It had taken him weeks of seducing her on a level that he hadn't had to employ for years. If ever.

After she'd revealed herself so spectacularly, and walked out of his hospital room, he'd put it down to being part of her act, but now he had to acknowledge that she *had* been a virgin. She hadn't lied about that. At least.

He was about to head up the stairs when a smell caught at his nostrils. A very distinctive smell. Delicious. Mouth-watering. Evocative of his childhood.

He went towards the kitchen, expecting to find Dominique cooking, but when he opened the door it took a second for his eyes to take in the scene.

Lara was bent down at the open oven door, taking something out. She was dressed in jeans and a loose shirt. Bare feet. Her hair was up in a messy knot, and as she turned around with the dish in her hands he saw how the buttons of the shirt were fastened low enough to give a tantalising glimpse of cleavage.

Tendrils of hair framed her face and flushed cheeks. He heard the music. Some silly pop tune. Then realised that Lara was smiling, bending down to sniff the food in the dish. Lasagne, he guessed. It reminded him of the famous lasagne his *nonna* used to make when he was small, hurtling him back in time.

Ciro was rendered mute and frozen, because he couldn't deny the appeal of the scene, nor that it had already existed in the deepest recesses of his psyche, even as he would have denied ever wanting such a domestic scenario in his life. At least until he'd met Lara that first time around and suddenly his perspective had shifted to allow such things to exist.

She'd cooked for him one evening; a spaghetti *vongole*. So mouthwatering that he could still recall how it had tasted, and the look of uncertainty on her face until he'd declared it delicious.

He'd totally forgotten about that until now.

At that second she looked up at him, catching him in a moment between past and present. Between who this woman was and who she wasn't.

Ciro felt as if there was a spotlight on his head, exposing every flaw—and not just the very physical ones. His scar felt itchy now, compounding his sense of dislocation and exposure. The scar that didn't seem to bother her in the slightest.

'What do you think you're doing?'

Lara looked as frozen as he felt. 'Cooking.'

'For who? Your imaginary friends?'

Ciro didn't have to see the rush of colour into Lara's cheeks to know he was being a bastard, but this whole scenario was unacceptable to him on a level that he really didn't want to investigate too closely.

Lara cursed herself for having given in to this urge to do something so domestic, but she refused to let Ciro's palpable disapproval intimidate her. She wouldn't let another man tell her she couldn't cook.

'It's lasagne, Ciro, not some subversive act.'

A suspicious look came over his face as he advanced into the kitchen. 'Why are you doing it, then? Angling to forge a more permanent position in my life by showcasing your domestic skills? As if they might hide your true nature?'

Lara pushed the dish away from the edge of the island, curbing the urge to lift it up and throw it at Ciro's cynical head. She said through gritted teeth, 'I really hadn't thought about it too much. I merely wanted to cook. It's Dominique's night off—how else am I going to feed myself?'

Ciro was so close now that Lara could see his long eyelashes casting shadows on his cheeks. They should have diminished his extreme masculinity. They didn't.

Feeling exasperated now, as well as jittery that Ciro was so close, Lara said, 'You've been out for dinner every night, Ciro. Did you really expect that I'd be sitting here pining away for your company?'

He flushed as if she'd hit a nerve. 'Clearly I made a mistake in not taking you along to those dinners with me.'

Lara started backing away around the kitchen island, her jitteriness increasing as Ciro advanced. 'No, it's fine—honestly. I know those things are work-related...not interesting. I'd only cramp your style.'

Then, as if she hadn't spoken, Ciro said almost musingly, 'I had no idea you liked going to bed so early. I seem to remember you telling me that you loved the night-time—after midnight, when everyone else is asleep and the world is finally quiet and at peace.'

Now Lara flushed. He'd remembered that romantic stroll when he'd taken her through deserted Florentine squares under the moonlight? She'd been such a sap, believing he wanted to hear all her silly chattering about everything and anything.

He waved a hand. 'None of that's important. There's only one thing I'm interested in right now, and that's repairing an area of our marriage that seems to have become neglected, thanks to my workload and your proclivity for early nights.'

Lara could see the explicit gleam in his eye and felt herself responding as if she literally had no agency over her own body.

'Actually, I think this week is a good example of how this marriage will succeed,' she blurted out with a sense of desperation. 'You know, if you want to take a mistress then please go right ahead. It might be better, actually, if we're to keep things clear and separate. After all, my worth is only really in helping you to network.'

Ciro barked out a laugh and shook his head.

'Take a mistress and give you grounds for divorce? I don't think so, *cara mia*. And you do yourself down. Your worth isn't only for your social standing and connections—it's also in the place where I want you right now.'

Lara stopped moving, feeling a sense of inevitability washing over her that, treacherously, she didn't fight. 'Where's that?'

Ciro came and stood in front of her. 'My bed...under me.'

The lasagne growing cool on the island was forgotten. Everything was distilled down to this moment and the way Ciro was looking at her.

He reached out and she felt air caress her skin. He was undoing her shirt and she slapped at his hands. 'Stop! What if someone comes in?'

Ciro was spreading her shirt apart now, his hands spanning her waist. She was finding it hard to focus as he tugged her forward.

'Dominique isn't here and Nigel has gone home. I passed him on my way in.'

Lara knew all that. They were entirely alone in this vast townhouse. She was so close to his body now that she could smell his scent. It reminded her of Sicily, of the sun baking the ground and something far more sensual and musky. *Him*.

She knew he was distracting her, and also punishing her on some level for having had the temerity to bring domesticity into this situation, but all she could think about was how she had denied herself his touch all week.

His head was coming closer, and Lara fought a tiny pathetic internal battle before she gave up and allowed Ciro's mouth to capture hers. He pressed her back against the island but Lara didn't even notice. Nor did she notice when Ciro pulled off her shirt and undid her bra, freeing her breasts into his hands, bringing her nipples to stinging life.

She squirmed against him, instinctively seeking flesh-on-flesh contact. He smiled against her mouth and Lara felt it, just as he broke the kiss and trailed his mouth down over her jaw and her chest to her breasts, tipping up first one and then the other, so that he could feast on them, sucking and licking and biting gently, causing a rush of hot blood to flow between Lara's legs, damp and hot.

Suddenly she was being lifted into Ciro's arms and he was carrying her out of the kitchen and up through the house. Lara's breathing was uneven. She realised she was bare from the waist up, but she could feel no shame, only a sense of rising desperation.

When they got to Ciro's bedroom he shed his clothes with indecent haste. Lara was equally ready, pulling off her jeans and panties, her skin prickling with need as she lay back and took in the sight of Ciro standing proudly by the bed, every muscle bulging and taut as he rolled protection on.

She wanted to weep because she was so ready. It made a mockery of the nights when she'd feigned sleep and believed herself to have scored some kind of victory. It had been a pyrrhic victory. Empty.

Ciro came down on the bed by Lara and she bit her lip. He put a thumb there, tugging her lip free, before claiming her mouth in a drugging, time-altering kiss. Ciro's hands explored every inch of her body until she was incoherent with need, past the point of begging.

But he knew. Of course he knew. Because he was the devil.

He settled his body between her spread legs, and in the same moment that he thrust deep, to the very core of where she ached most, he took her mouth and absorbed her hoarse cry of relief.

It was fast and furious. Lara reached her peak in a blinding rush of pleasure so intense she blacked out for a moment. Ciro's body locked tight a moment after, his huge powerful frame struggling to contain his own climax. It gave Lara some small measure of satisfaction to see his features twisted in an agony of pleasure as deep shudders racked his frame.

One thing was clear in her mind before a satisfaction-induced coma took her over. Ciro had just demonstrated very clearly where the parameters of this marriage lay: in the bedroom and on the social circuit. Not in the kitchen.

When Lara woke the next morning she was back in her own bed. She really hated it that Ciro did that. *What was he afraid of?* she grumbled to herself. Was he afraid he'd wake up and she'd have spun a web around his body, turning him into a prisoner?

The image gave her more than a little dart of satisfaction. The thought of Ciro being totally at her mercy…

She didn't hear any sounds coming from his bedroom and checked the time, realising that Ciro would have gone to the office already.

After showering and dressing she went downstairs to find Dominique in the kitchen. The woman turned around and smiled widely, and it was only at that moment that Lara had a mortifying flashback and saw her shirt and bra neatly folded on a chair near the door.

She grabbed them, her face burning, gabbling an apology, but the older woman put up a hand.

'Don't apologise. It's your home. I might have been married for twenty years, but I do remember what that first heady year was like.'

Lara smiled weakly, welcoming the change in subject when Dominique said, 'The lasagne— did you cook it? It smells delicious. I've put it in the fridge but I can freeze it if you like.'

Lara had been taught a comprehensive and very effective lesson last night in not expecting to see Ciro sitting down to a home-cooked meal any time soon, so she said, 'Actually, do you want to take it home with you this evening for you and your family? I thought we'd have a chance to eat it but we won't.'

Dominique reached for something and handed a folded card to Lara. 'That reminds me—Ciro left this for you. And, yes, I'd love to take the lasagne home if you're sure that's all right? It'll save me cooking!'

Lara smiled and retreated from the kitchen. 'Of course. I hope you enjoy it.'

She looked at the card once she was out of sight. The handwriting was strong and slashing.

Be ready to leave for a function at five this evening. Dress for black tie.

No, she could be under no illusions now as to where her role lay.

On her back and at Ciro's side as his trophy wife.

Ciro's driver came for Lara at five. She checked her appearance in the mirror of the hall one last time. The long sleeveless black dress had a lace bodice and a high collar. She'd pulled her hair back into a sleek ponytail and kept jewellery and make-up to a minimum.

The car made its way through the London traffic to one of the city's most iconic museums. She saw Ciro before he saw her in the car. He was standing by the kerb, where cars were disgorging people in glittering finery.

For a moment Lara just drank him in, in his classic tuxedo. He must have changed at the office. He was utterly mesmerising. She could see other women doing double-takes.

Then he saw the car and she saw tension come into his form. She felt a pang. They might combust in bed, but he still resented her presence out of it. Even if he did need her.

The car drew to a stop and Lara gathered herself as Ciro opened the door and helped her out. Even her hand in his was enough to cause a seismic reaction in her body. But she felt shy after what had happened last night.

Ciro said, 'You look beautiful.'

She glanced at him, embarrassed. 'Thank you. You look very smart.'

A small smile tipped up his mouth. 'Smart? I don't think I've been called that before.'

Lara felt hot. No... Ciro's lovers would have twined themselves around him and whispered into his ear that he was magnificent. Gorgeous. Sexy.

She felt gauche, but he was taking her elbow in his hand and leading her towards the throng of people entering the huge museum near Kensington Gardens, one of London's most exclusive addresses.

It was only when they were seated that Lara realised it was a banquet dinner to honour three charities. One of which had Ciro Sant'Angelo's name on it.

She read the blurb on the brochure.

The Face Forward Charity. Founded by Ciro Sant'Angelo after a kidnapping ordeal left him facially disfigured.

There was an interview with Ciro in which he explained that after his injury he'd realised that any physical disfigurement, not just facial, was something that affected millions of people. And that a lot of disfigurement came about due to birth defects, injuries of some kind—whether through accident, war or gangs—or domestic violence.

His mission statement was that no one should ever be made to feel 'less' because of their disfigurement. His charity offered a wide range of treatments, ranging from plastic surgery to rehabilitation and counselling, to help people afflicted. To help them move on with their lives.

Lara looked at Ciro. She was seated on his right-hand side and his scar seemed to stand out even more this evening. A statement.

He glanced at her and arched a brow. She felt hurt that he hadn't mentioned this before. 'I didn't know you'd set up a charity.'

He shrugged minutely. 'I didn't think it relevant to tell you.'

Something deeper than hurt bloomed inside Lara then. Something she couldn't even really articulate.

She stood up abruptly, just as they were serving the starters, and almost knocked over the waiter behind her. Apologising, she fled from the room, upset and embarrassed.

Once outside, in the now empty foyer, she stopped. She cursed herself for bolting like that. The last thing Ciro would want was for people's attention to be drawn to them.

She heard heavy footsteps behind her. Ciro caught her arm, swinging her around. 'What the hell, Lara?'

She pulled free, her anger and hurt surging again at the irritated look on his face. 'I know you don't like me very much, Ciro, but we're married now. The least you could have done is tell me what this evening is about. *You're* the one concerned with appearances. How do you think it would look if someone struck up a conversation with me about your charity which I know nothing about?'

Ciro felt a constriction in his chest. Lara was right. But he hadn't neglected to tell her about it in a conscious effort not to include her. He hadn't told her because he didn't find it easy to mention the kidnapping. Even now. Even here, where he was in public and talking about something that had arisen out of that experience.

Lara looked...*hurt*. And then she said, 'I was there too, you know. I didn't experience what you experienced, and I'm so sorry that you went through what you did. But they took me too, Ciro. So I do have some idea of what you went through, even if it's only very superficial. I might not have any physical scars to prove I had that experience, but I had it.'

She turned and went to walk back into the room, but Ciro caught her arm again. For the first time, he felt the balance of power between them shift slightly.

She looked at him, her full mouth set in a line. Her jaw tight.

'You're right,' he said, and the words came easier than he might have expected. 'I should have told you—and, yes, you *were* there too.'

'Thank you.'

Ciro realised in that moment that she had all the regal bearing and grace of royalty, and something inside him was inexplicably humbled. She'd been right to call him out on this. And he wasn't used to being in the wrong. It was not a sensation he'd expected to feel in the presence of Lara.

Lara felt shaky after confronting Ciro, but his

apology defused her anger. She realised now that she'd been hurt because she'd felt left out, which was ridiculous when Ciro had set up the charity well before they'd met again.

After the meal people got up to give speeches, and Lara was a little stunned when Ciro was introduced and he got up to go to the podium. He was a commanding presence. The crowd seemed far more hushed when he spoke. And how could she blame them? He stood out.

His scar also stood out, in a white ridged line down the right side of his face. Most people probably wouldn't even notice his missing finger, too transfixed by that scar.

He spoke passionately about the psychological effects of being scarred and how, with pioneering plastic surgery treatments, people could have the option of going on to live scar-free lives. Especially children.

There was a slideshow of images of some of the children and people his charity had helped so far, and Lara had tears in her eyes by the time he was finished.

When he came back to the table Lara felt

humbled. She'd seen a new depth to Ciro to-night. Ever since she'd met him he'd always projected a charming, carefree attitude to life. He was someone who'd been graced with good looks, wealth and intellect. Taken for granted—as his due. Not any more. That much was blatantly obvious.

When they had returned to the townhouse Lara said, 'I think what you're doing is amazing. If there's ever anything I can do… I'd like to be involved.'

Ciro turned to face her. 'There is something you can do…right now.'

He took her hand and tugged her towards him.

Instant heat flooded Lara's body at the explicit gleam in his eyes. 'Ciro…' she said weakly.

'Lara…' he said, and then he stopped any more words by fusing his mouth to hers.

It was only much later, when Lara was back in her own bed, her body still tingling in the aftermath of extreme pleasure, that she realised he'd effectively dismissed her desire to help with the charity.

Clearly it was an arena, along with the kitchen, that she wasn't allowed to enter. Which only made Lara determined to do something about it.

CHAPTER SEVEN

'SHE'S *WHERE*?'

Ciro stood up from his chair and stalked over to the window, which took in a view of the Thames snaking through London.

The voice on the other end of the phone sounded nervous, 'Er...she's in one of the Face Forward charity shops, boss. It looks like she's helping with the display in the window.'

Ciro was terse. 'Send me a video and stay with her until she leaves.'

About a minute later there was a *ping* on his phone and he played the video. There was Lara, in jeans and a sweatshirt, hair pulled back, helping to dress and accessorise a mannequin in the window of one of his charity's shops on the King's Road.

She looked about sixteen. He saw her turn and smile broadly at a young staff member.

She looked…*happy*. Happier than he'd seen her since they'd met again.

Something dark settled into his chest. A heavy weight. And confusion. Who the hell was she doing this for? What was she up to?

'What do you mean, what was I up to? *Nothing!* I wanted to prove that I was serious about helping with the charity. Or do you expect me to sit around all day waiting for the moment you decide to dress me up and take me out as your trophy wife?'

Ciro had been festering all day and he'd come home in a black mood. Which had got even blacker when he'd found Lara in the kitchen again, cooking.

'I thought I told you that I don't expect you to cook?'

She smiled sweetly at him, which made his blood boil even more, because it only reminded him of the very real smile he'd seen on that video earlier.

'I'm not cooking for you. I'm cooking for me. And Dominique. She can take the leftovers for her and Bill.'

'Bill?'

'Her husband. He's not well.'

'And you know this...*how*?'

Lara looked at him now as if he was a bit dense. 'Because I have conversations with her.'

Ciro was aware that he was being totally irrational and ridiculous. His wife was cooking in the kitchen. Most men would be ecstatic. Especially as it smelt so delicious.

Lara said, 'I know there's nothing on tonight, thanks to the helpful events calendar your assistant installed in the phone you gave me. Unless that's changed?' She suddenly looked less happy.

'No,' Ciro bit out. 'It hasn't changed. The evening is free.'

'Well,' Lara said, sounding eminently reasonable, and far calmer than Ciro felt, 'have you made plans for dinner or would you like to join me? It's *boeuf bourguignon*.'

Ciro forced himself to stop being ridiculous. He had no idea what Lara was up to with this little charade—helping at the charity shop and revealing her domestic goddess side—but he wasn't foolish enough to cut off his nose to spite his face.

'That would be nice, thank you. I'll have a shower and join you.'

Ciro left and Lara took a deep breath. She regretted cooking now. Dominique had left a perfectly serviceable stew she could have heated up, but she'd needed the ritual of cooking to centre herself.

She guessed Ciro's security guy would have been on the phone to him earlier, about her going to the charity shop, and she'd expected his suspicious mind to spin it into something nefarious.

She knew he expected her to be like some kind of ice princess, waiting obediently for his instructions, but since they'd begun sleeping together it was harder and harder to maintain that kind of façade. And any emotional distance.

So Ciro could just *be* perplexed and suspicious. He didn't really care who she was, after all. So why not be herself?

The following morning Lara was surprised to see Ciro in the kitchen, chatting to Dominique over a cup of coffee. She felt exposed when she thought of the previous evening, and how Ciro had quickly and efficiently dispensed with dinner so that he could remind Lara of one of her primary functions in this marriage. Being in his bed.

He'd said it to her again as they'd finished eating. 'I really don't expect you to be in the kitchen, Lara.'

She shrugged. 'I know I don't have to do it, but I like it.'

He'd looked at her as if she'd spoken in some kind of riddle and then, when she'd been getting up to clear the plates, he'd pulled her down onto his lap. 'I'm drawing the line here. You do *not* clear up.'

Lara was blushing now because she was thinking of Dominique finding their detritus. Again. But the woman was looking twinkly-eyed. The inevitable effect of Ciro on most people.

She wondered what Dominique thought of their separate beds...

Ciro looked at her then. 'You need to pack. We're leaving for New York this morning.

Some business has been moved forward. We'll be there a couple of weeks. Don't worry too much about what to bring—a stylist will stock your wardrobe there. They've been given a list of the functions we're due to attend.'

Ciro walked out the kitchen with his coffee cup and Dominique sighed volubly. 'What I wouldn't give to have my wardrobe stocked for me.'

Lara forced a smile and desisted from saying something trite. She knew she was incredibly lucky. Even if it *did* feel as though she were a bird in a gilded cage.

As she packed her modest suitcase a little later she told herself she was being ridiculous to suspect that Ciro had brought forward the New York trip to keep her in her place, because things were getting a little too domesticated in London.

Ciro seemed to be in a state of permanent frustration around Lara. He watched her broodingly from his side of the private plane as she did a crossword puzzle. A pen was between her teeth and her brow was furrowed. Why wasn't she flicking through a magazine? Or drinking champagne? Or trying to seduce him?

He turned away, angry that he couldn't seem to focus on his own work. And also angry because he'd acted impulsively, deciding to come to New York ahead of schedule purely because the previous night and that dinner had impacted on him somewhere he didn't like to investigate.

He hadn't married Lara so she could be of actual help in any aspect of his life other than in the social arena. And in his bed. Yet she was starting to inhabit more parts of his life than he liked to admit.

Apart from the dinner last night he'd noticed soft touches around the house in London. Flowers. Throws. Shoes left discarded. Unintentional little feminine touches. Not even anything concrete he could point to.

Ciro had never lived with a woman. Lara would have been the first and she was still the first. In spite of what had happened.

Because of what had happened.

He found that as much as it made him feel exposed and discombobulated he couldn't say that he didn't like it. He just hadn't counted on

Lara's softness. Her ability to converse with the staff. Her...*niceness.*

She'd been nice before. And then she'd changed. So he wouldn't believe it. He had to believe she was up to something. It was easier.

Lara could feel Ciro's eyes on her. She could almost hear his brain whirring. She knew how he worked. He problem-solved. And she was a problem because she wasn't behaving as he thought she should. As he thought the Lara who had rejected him should.

She felt something well up inside her. The urge to just turn around and let it all spill out. The full truth about her treacherous uncle. About what had happened. She even opened her mouth and turned to Ciro...and then promptly shut it again.

His head was thrown back and his eyes were closed. She'd never seen him asleep. He looked no less formidable.

The urge to talk drained and faded. It would be self-serving. She might want to be absolved of all her sins in his eyes, but was she really ready to face his disgust? He would get rid of her immediately, of that she had no doubt. As it was, the ties binding them were incredibly fragile.

Ciro was so proud. It would kill him to know that she knew the truth about the kidnapping. That it had been done to him by *her* family. He would blame her. No doubt. *She* blamed herself. Why wouldn't he?

She got up from her chair and pulled a blanket over Ciro's body. Immediately his eyes opened and he caught her, bringing her down onto his lap. She was instantly breathless.

She looked at him accusingly. 'I thought you were asleep.'

'Are you finished pretending to be uninterested?'

She saw something in his eyes then—very fleeting. It almost looked like vulnerability.

Lara might have made some trite comment or pushed herself away from Ciro, fought to keep the distance between them, but instead she said, 'You're not a person who would ever inspire a lack of interest, Ciro.'

'That's more like it.'

He pulled her head down and kissed her.

Lara fought to retain a little bit of resistance,

but it was futile. Within minutes Ciro was carrying her through the cabin to the back of the plane, where the bed awaited.

New York felt different from London. Where London felt intimate, New York felt expansive and impersonal.

Ciro had a townhouse there too—which was some feat in a city full of soaring buildings and massive apartment blocks. It was nestled between two huge buildings by Central Park, on the Upper East Side.

His staff there were polite and impersonal. Lara couldn't imagine getting to know them all that well. And from the day they arrived she was sucked into a dizzying round of events and functions.

The days took on a rhythm. Ciro would get up and go to his office downtown. Lara would get up, have breakfast and then go to the park for a run. Invariably she found herself sitting on a bench watching other people—couples, dog-walkers, children and their nannies.

She saw a family one day—father, mother and two children. A boy and a girl. It made her heart ache, and she cursed Ciro for making that pain real again even as she denied to herself that she was still in love with him.

Their evenings were spent either at banquet dinners or less formal functions. Lara had lost count of all the people she'd met. There was no time here for cooking cosy dinners in the kitchen. It was as if Ciro was purposely not letting her have the opportunity.

But even he hadn't been able to complain when they'd been passing a famous pizza place a couple of nights ago and Lara had asked if they could stop. She'd been starving, and so, it turned out, had been Ciro, his driver and his security team. So they'd all stood around the high tables, eating slices of pizza. Ciro in his tuxedo with his bow tie undone and Lara in a glittering strapless silver sheath dress.

It had been a very private personal victory for Lara.

And then the nights...

Ciro would take her to bed in his room, shatter her into a million pieces over and over again and then deposit her back in her own bed. Sometimes Lara was glad, because the intimacy felt too raw. But other times she despised him for the way he seemed to find it so easy to despatch her.

His determination to keep her confined to the box in which he'd kept her since he'd married her was very apparent. She knew it wasn't a real marriage, but their physical intimacy was wearing her down and making it harder and harder to keep her guard up. And she hated him for that. Because he seemed totally impervious to it.

That evening they had yet another function to attend and Ciro knocked on Lara's door.

Feeling incredibly weary, she called out, 'I'm ready.'

He opened the door and came in, his dark gaze sweeping her up and down. It turned hot as he took in her light blue silk evening gown. It was one-shouldered, and fell in soft fluid folds around her body—which came to humming life under Ciro's assessing look. *Damn him.*

Her hair was up in a loose chignon and she'd chosen dangling diamond earrings. The only other jewellery she wore was her engagement and wedding rings.

'Stunning,' Ciro pronounced. And then, 'Let's go. The car is waiting.'

For a second Lara wanted to stamp her feet and refuse to follow him, but she swallowed the urge. This wasn't a real marriage. Ciro didn't care if she was feeling weary from the constant socialising. He didn't care because this was all about work for him—a means to an end. And essentially she was just an employee. With benefits.

At the function that evening—there had been so many of them that even Ciro felt as if all the faces and places were blurring into one mass of people—he felt disgruntled. When he had no reason to do so.

Lara was at his side, conversing in Spanish with a diplomat. She was fulfilling her role as corporate wife with absolute perfection. She wasn't behaving like a spoilt petulant princess, demanding attention, or moaning because her feet hurt from standing too long.

But he sensed it. Her discomfiture. He saw it

when she moved her weight from foot to foot, or when she winced slightly as someone shook her hand too hard. He saw it when she quickly masked a look of boredom. The same boredom he was feeling.

He'd seen it in her eyes earlier—a kind of fatigue along with the slightest of shadows under her eyes. After all, they weren't falling asleep until near dawn most nights.

Ciro had been feeling more and more reluctant to take Lara back to her own bed after making love to her, and was doing it out of sheer bloody-mindedness—so she didn't get ideas and think that their mind-blowing sex was leading to any deeper kind of intimacy.

She'd asked if they could stop on their way home the other night. For pizza. The gratitude on his staff's faces had made Ciro feel guilty about how hard he was working them. Not to mention the almost sexual look of pleasure on Lara's face as she'd bitten into a slice. It had been the best damn pizza he'd ever tasted. And he'd eaten pizza in Naples.

It had been fun. Unexpected. And it had reminded him so much of when he'd known Lara *before* that past and present had blurred painfully.

There were too many of those moments now. Moments that made him doubt his sanity. His memory.

Maybe that was why he'd insisted on such a punishing pace. So as not to give himself a chance to stop and think for a second.

'Do you think we could go now? I'm quite tired.'

Ciro looked around. He hadn't even noticed most of the other guests leaving. Lara looked pale, the shadows under her eyes more pronounced.

A dart of guilt lanced Ciro before he could stop it. 'Of course, let's go.'

They got outside and even he was grateful for the fresh air. He wondered if all this endless networking was really worth it. That would have shocked him if he'd thought it before.

Suddenly his thoughts came to a standstill as Lara stopped beside him and then darted towards a dark alleyway nearby. All he could see was her light blue dress disappearing like an aquamarine jewel into the dark night.

'What the…?'

Ciro flicked a hand to tell his security team that he would get her. As he walked towards the alleyway, though, he felt his insides curdle at the thought that she might be trying to run.

This was it. What she'd been up to.

He'd given her a credit card—maybe she'd just been biding her time. Maybe she'd met a man at one of these functions and devised a plan to escape with someone more charming than him. Someone who would offer her a lifetime of security and not just a year or six months. Someone who didn't have their tangled history…

But at that moment Lara appeared again, in the mouth of the alleyway, and he came to a stop at the same time as his irrational circling thoughts.

He frowned at the sight before him.

She was holding something in her arms against her chest. Something that was moving. Shaking uncontrollably. She came forward, her eyes huge and filled with compassion. 'It's a puppy… I heard it crying. It needs help. It's been attacked by someone, or another dog. It's bleeding.'

Ciro could see it now—an indeterminate bundle of matted hair and big wounded-looking eyes. Dark blood was running down Lara's dress along with muck and dirt. There was a streak of something dark along her cheek and he could smell the dog from here.

For a second he couldn't compute the scene. Lara, dressed in a couture gown, uncaring of the fact that she was holding a mangy dog covered in blood and filth.

'Please, Ciro, we need to take him to a vet. He'll die.'

A memory blasted Ciro at that moment. He'd been very small. Tiny. Holding his mother's hand as she'd walked along the street. Which had been odd, because generally she hadn't taken him with her anywhere, not liking to take the risk that he would do something to show her up in public.

But on this day he'd been with her, and as they'd passed a side street he'd seen some older boys pelting a cowering dog with stones. He'd stopped dead, eyes wide on the awful scene. He could remember trying to call *Mamma!* but his mouth wouldn't work. Eventually she'd stopped and demanded to know why he wouldn't move.

He had pointed his finger, horrified at what he was witnessing. Such cruelty. He'd looked up at her, tears filling his eyes, willing her to do something. But she had taken one look, then gripped his hand so tightly it had hurt and dragged him away.

The piteous yelps of that dog had stayed with him for a long time. And he'd forgotten about it until this moment.

'Ciro…?'

He moved. 'Of course. Here—let me take him.'

She clutched the animal to her. 'No, it's fine. He's not heavy. There's no point two of us getting dirty.'

Ciro just looked at her. And then he said, 'Fine. We'll find the closest vet.'

Lara got into the back of the car carefully, cradling the bony body of the dog, which was still shaking pitifully. There was no way she could have ignored the distinctive crying once she'd heard it. She adored dogs.

She heard Ciro on the phone, asking someone to find them a vet and send directions immediately. She imagined a minion somewhere jumping to attention.

Ciro's phone rang seconds later and he listened for a second before rattling off an address to the driver.

He said to Lara, 'We'll be at the vet's in ten minutes—they're expecting us.'

'Thank you. I'm sorry, but I couldn't just…'

'It's fine.' Ciro's voice was clipped.

Lara said, 'If you want you can just leave me at the vet with the dog… I can call a taxi to get home.'

Ciro looked at her. She could see the dark pools of his eyes in the gloom of the back of the car.

'Don't be ridiculous. I'll wait.'

After that Lara stayed silent, willing the dog to survive. When they got to the vet Ciro insisted on taking the dog into his arms, and Lara was surprised to hear him crooning softly to it in Italian, evidently not minding about getting dirty himself.

There was a team waiting when they got

inside—the power of Ciro's wealth and influence—and the dog was whisked away to be assessed. Lara felt something warm settle around her shoulders and looked up. Ciro had given her his jacket. She realised that it was chilly inside, with the air-conditioning on, and she'd been shivering.

'Coffee?'

She nodded, and watched as Ciro went to the machine provided for clients. He handed her a coffee and took a sip of his own. It was only then that Lara caught a glimpse of herself in the reflection of a window and winced inwardly. Her hair was coming down on one side and she had streaks of dirt all over her face and chest. And her dress was ruined.

She gestured with her free hand. 'I'm sorry... I didn't mean to ruin the dress.'

Ciro looked at her curiously. 'It's not as if you would have worn it again.'

She thought of how much a dress like this might have fetched in an online auction, like when she'd been reduced to selling her clothes while married to Henry Winterborne. She couldn't ever imagine telling Ciro that story. He wouldn't believe her.

She said, 'Of course not,' and sat down on a plastic chair, the adrenalin leaving her system. They were the only people at the vets. The harsh fluorescent lighting barely dented Ciro's intensely gorgeous looks. He caught her eye and she looked away hastily, in case he saw something on her face. She felt exposed after her impetuous action. Less able to try and erect the emotional barriers between her and Ciro.

If she ever had been able to.

'Lara…'

Reluctantly she looked at him.

He shook his head. 'Sometimes you just… confound me. I think I know exactly who you are and then—'

At that moment there was a noise and Ciro stopped talking. Lara welcomed the distraction, not sure if she wanted to know what Ciro had been about to say.

The vet walked in and looked at them both before saying, 'Well, he is a she and it's lucky you found her when you did. She wouldn't have survived much longer. She's about five months old and as far as we can tell she hasn't been microchipped. She's probably from a stray litter or got dumped.'

Lara said, 'Is she okay?'

The vet nodded. 'She'll be fine—thanks to you for bringing her in. She's obviously been in a scrap, but it's just cuts and bruises. Nothing too serious. She needs some TLC and some food. We can microchip her and keep her in overnight to clean her up, then you can take her home tomorrow, if you like?' He must have seen something on their faces because then he said, 'I'm sorry, I just assumed you'd want to keep her, but I can see I shouldn't have.'

Lara didn't want to look at Ciro, but all of a sudden it seemed of paramount importance that she got to keep the dog. As if something hinged on this very decision.

Without looking at Ciro, she said, 'I'd like to keep her.'

The vet looked at Ciro, who must have nodded or something, because he said, 'That's good. Thank you.' The vet was just turning to leave and then he said, 'You should probably think of a name.'

Lara sneaked a look at Ciro, who was expressionless. But she could see his tight jaw.

'We'll let you know,' he said.

The vet left and Lara said, 'If you don't want to keep her I'll look after her and take her with me when I leave. You won't even know she's there.'

She. Her.

As if they were discussing a person.

Ciro wasn't sure why, but he had an almost visceral urge *not* to take this puppy. A puppy smacked of domesticity. Longevity. Attachment.

'It's fine. You can keep her.'

Ciro told himself that Lara would soon tire of the dog and then he would arrange for it to go to a new home. A home with a family who would appreciate it.

But even as he thought that he felt some resistance inside him. He was losing it. Seeing how Lara had been with the dog had made him feel as if he was standing on shifting sands.

'Thank you.'

'Let's go.'

Lara walked out ahead of Ciro, his jacket

dwarfing her slender shoulders. She should have looked ridiculous. Her hair was all over the place and she was smeared in dubious-smelling substances. Not to mention the blood. Yet she seemed oblivious to it.

When they were in the back of the car Lara said, 'Sorry—I know I stink.'

Ciro looked at her in the dim light. Even as dishevelled as she was, she was stunning. More so, if possible. As if this act of humanity had added some quality to her beauty.

'I wouldn't have had you down as a dog-lover.'

Her mouth curved into a small smile. 'My parents got a rescue Labrador puppy when I was just a toddler. We called her Poppy, we were inseparable.'

'What happened to her?'

The smile faded. 'After my parents and brother died my uncle had her put down. She was old… She probably only had another year at the most.'

Ciro absorbed that nugget of information. He could hear the emotion she was trying to hide in her voice.

'Have you thought of a name for this one?'

She turned to look at him and he could see the gratitude in her eyes. He really didn't want it to affect him, but it did. He couldn't imagine another woman looking so pleased about taking on a mongrel of dubious parentage.

'Maybe Hero? I've always liked that name. After the Greek myth.'

The fact that Hero had been a virgin priestess wasn't lost on Ciro, but he only said, 'Fine. Whatever you want. She's your dog.'

When they arrived back at the house Lara made a face and gestured to her clothes. 'I should clean myself up.'

She handed Ciro his jacket. He took it, and there was something vulnerable about the way Lara looked. He had a memory flash of having her ripped out of his arms by the kidnappers and thrown from the van to the side of the road. She'd been dishevelled then too. And the look of terror on her face had matched the terror he'd felt but had been desperate not to show.

'Of course,' he said tersely. 'Go to bed, Lara, it's been a long night.'

Ciro went into the reception room and

dropped his jacket on a chair, loosening his bow tie. Except he knew it wasn't the fault of his tie that he felt constricted. It was something far more complicated.

He poured himself a whisky and downed the shot in one go, hoping to burn away the questions buzzing in his head. Along with the unwelcome memories.

He forced his mind away from the past and the image of Lara's terror-stricken face to think of her as she was now—standing under a shower, naked. With rivulets of water streaming down over her curves, her nipples hard and pebbled. The soft curls between her legs would be wet, as wet as she always was when he touched her there—

Dio! He had a wife, willing and hot for him, one floor above his head, and he was down here, torturing himself, when he could be burying himself inside her and forgetting about everything except the release she offered.

Ciro slammed down the glass and went upstairs, taking two stairs at a time. When he got to Lara's bedroom door he stopped, his sense of urgency suddenly diminishing when he thought of how vulnerable she'd looked. What she'd told him about her family dog. Her uncle had had her put down. Just after her family had been taken from her.

Ciro had had his hand lifted, as if to knock on her door, but he curled it into a fist now, and walked away.

CHAPTER EIGHT

IT SEEMED TO take an age for Lara to fall asleep. She could have sworn she heard Ciro outside her bedroom, and even as she'd longed for him to come in she'd known that if he did she wasn't sure she'd be able to maintain the façade that she was as cool and impervious to their intimacy as he was.

So when he didn't appear in her doorway she couldn't help a tiny dart of relief.

She slept fitfully, and when she woke at some point in the night she wasn't sure if she'd been asleep for hours, or had only just fallen asleep.

And then she heard it—the sound that must have woken her. A shout. A guttural shout drawn from the very depths of someone's soul.

Ciro.

The tiny hairs stood up all over Lara's body as he shouted again—something indeterminate. Half English, half Italian. She realised she was getting out of bed before she'd even decided to do so, and she went to the adjoining door to Ciro's room.

And then he unleashed a cry that she did understand.

'No—stop!'

Lara didn't hesitate. She opened the door and flew into Ciro's room, where he was thrashing in the bed. Naked. A sheet was tangled around his hips and legs, and his hands were balled into fists at his sides. His skin was sheened with sweat. His hair was damp.

Lara went into the bathroom and soaked a cloth with cold water. She brought it back and sat beside Ciro on the bed, pressing the damp cloth to his forehead. She desperately wanted to ease his pain without waking him, if she could help it. She knew he wouldn't thank her for seeing him in such a vulnerable state.

But then one of his hands caught her wrist and suddenly she was looking down into wide open dark eyes. She held her breath. He was breathing as if he'd run a marathon.

'Ciro…?' Lara whispered. 'You were dreaming…'

With a sudden move Ciro had Lara flat on her back and was looming over her, both her wrists caught in his hands. Now *she* was breathing as if she'd been running. She didn't know if he was asleep or awake and he looked crazed. Yet she wasn't scared. She knew he wouldn't hurt her. Even like this.

Ciro was still reeling from the nightmare. So vivid he could still taste it on his tongue. Acrid. He wasn't even sure where he was. All he could see were Lara's huge blue eyes. Soft and full of the same emotion she'd had in them earlier when she'd held the dog. Pity... No, not pity. Compassion.

It impacted Ciro deep inside, and he felt a desperate need to transmute the effects of the nightmare into something much more tangible. He could feel her body against his, all lithe and soft like silk. The press of her breasts...the cradle of her hips.

He was so hard it hurt. Hard and aching. And not just in his body. In his chest, where he felt tight.

He took his hands off her wrists and put them either side of her head. 'I need you, Lara. Right here, right now, and I can't promise to be gentle. So if you want to go, go now.'

I need this. I need you.

He didn't say the words but they beat so heavily in his brain he wondered if he had said them out loud.

Lara reached up and wound her arms around his neck, bringing her body into close contact with his. 'Take me,' she said, 'I'm yours.'

And in that moment, Lara knew she was done for. She felt Ciro's need as clearly as if it was hers. And all she wanted to do was assuage his pain. She loved him. She still loved him. Had always loved him. Would always love him.

Ciro waited a beat, as if making sure that Lara knew what she was doing, and then with studied deliberation he put his hand to her silky nightgown and ripped it from top to bottom. It fell apart, baring her to his gaze, and Lara found herself revelling in it. She felt the ferocity Ciro felt—it thrummed through her in waves of need, building and building.

Ciro's dark gaze devoured her body and his hands moulded her every curve. His tongue laved her and with big hands he spread her legs so he could taste her there, making her cry out loud when he found and sucked on that little ball of nerves at the centre of her body.

She lifted her head, hardly able to see straight. She was sheened with sweat now too. 'Ciro, I can't wait…please.'

He reached for something and she saw him roll protection onto his length. For the first time Lara wished there could be nothing between them—but this marriage wasn't about that. Procreation. It was just about…*this*… She hissed out as Ciro joined their bodies with one cataclysmic thrust.

He was remorseless, using every skill he had to prolong and delay the pinnacle. At one point he withdrew from Lara, and she let out a pitiful-sounding mewl, but he rolled onto his back and urged her to sit astride him, saying roughly, 'I want to see you.'

Lara put her thighs either side of his hips and came up on her knees. She felt Ciro take himself in his hand, and then he guided her down onto his stiff length. She came down slowly, experimentally, savouring the exquisite sensation of Ciro feeding his length into her, and then he put his hands on her hips. 'Take me, *cara mia*…all of me.'

Lara soon found her rhythm, her slick body moving up and down on his, excitement building at her core, making her move faster. The pinnacle was still elusive, though, and she was almost crying with frustration as Ciro clamped his hands on her hips and held her still so that he could pump up into her body.

He pulled her down, finding her breast and sucking her nipple into his mouth as the first wave of the crescendo broke Lara into a million pieces. It went on and on, like waves endlessly crashing against the shore, until she was limp and spent and hollowed out.

In the seconds afterwards it was as if an explosion had just occurred. Her ears were ringing and she wasn't sure if she was still in one piece.

Her body and Ciro's were still intimately joined. She lay on him, exhausted but satisfied, her mouth resting on the hectic pulsepoint at the bottom of his neck, and that was all she remembered before she fell into a blissful dark oblivion.

* * *

When Lara woke she realised she was still in Ciro's bed. Dawn was breaking outside. He lay beside her on his back, one arm flung over his head, the other on his chest. Her gaze drifted down over hard pecs to the dark curls where his masculinity was still gloriously impressive, even in sleep.

She knew she should leave because he would soon return her to her room. She wondered with a pang if he'd ever let a woman spend the whole night in his bed.

She was sitting up when Ciro's hand caught her arm. 'Where do you think you're going?'

Lara's heart thumped. 'Back to my own bed.'

'Don't. Stay here.'

Lara looked at Ciro. His eyes were still closed. Maybe he wasn't even awake, so wasn't aware of what he was saying. She lay down carefully and he rolled towards her, trapping her with a leg over hers. She felt him stir against her. He opened his eyes.

A bubble of emotion rose up in her as she took in Ciro's stubbled face and messy hair. Without thinking she reached out and touched his scar gently, running her finger down the ridged length.

'Does it hurt?'

'Only sometimes… It doesn't hurt… It feels tight.'

'You were never tempted to get it removed? Like the people you help with your charity?'

His mouth firmed. 'No. I think it's important for people to see it—to know that if they want to live with their scars, it's okay. And it's a reminder.'

Lara was touched by his sentiment. Then she frowned. 'A reminder of the kidnapping…? Why would you want that?'

'Not that, specifically, but it's a reminder that I'm not as infallible as I once believed. And it's a reminder not to trust anyone.'

Including me, Lara thought.

Facing him like this in the half-light, with no sounds coming from outside, made her feel otherworldly. As if they were in some sort of cocoon.

'The dream you were having last night…'

Ciro rolled onto his back again. 'It was a nightmare.'

Hesitantly Lara asked, 'About the kidnapping?'

He nodded, clearly uncomfortable. He probably saw it as a sign of weakness.

'I had them too,' Lara said.

Ciro looked at her.

'For months afterwards. The same one, over and over again… The hoods being put over our heads, then taken off. Realising we were in that van with those men. Being ripped out of your arms…left at the side of the road—' She stopped, shivering at the memory.

Ciro reached for her and hauled her into his arms. He said, 'I would never let that happen again—do you hear me?'

Lara looked at him, saw the determination on his face. She nodded. 'I believe you.'

There was something incredibly fragile about the moment. And then Ciro hauled her even closer and kissed her. Their bodies moved together in the dawn as they reached for each other and their breath quickened. This was nothing like the ferocity of last night—it was slow and sensuous, and so tender that Lara had to keep her eyes closed for fear that Ciro would see how close to tears she was.

'Working from home again?'

Ciro looked at Lara and raised a brow, but there was no edginess to his expression. 'Do I need to ask permission?' he said.

Lara shook her head and helped herself to some of the salad which had been laid out on the terrace at the back of the house by the house-keeper. Ciro had been joining her for lunch the past few days. It had been a week since that tumultuous night, and since then Ciro hadn't taken her back to her own bedroom once. They woke up together, and usually made love again in the morning.

But Lara knew it was dangerous territory to believe anything was changing.

Ciro sat down and helped himself to some salad and bread. The housekeeper came out and poured them some wine.

There was a mewling cry from down below and Lara looked down to see Hero, looking up at her with huge liquid brown eyes. It turned out that she was been a cross between a whippet and something else. Cleaned up, and getting fatter by the day, she wasn't a pretty dog by any means—but she was adorable, mainly white with brown patches. The vet had said that he figured she was crossed with a Jack Russell.

A couple of times Lara had gone searching for her, only to find her curled up at Ciro's feet in his study. He'd pretended not to have noticed her, and when Lara had carried her out she'd whispered into her fur, 'I don't blame you, sweetheart. I know how it feels.'

Hero would lick her face, as if in commiseration for the fact that they were both in thrall to Ciro Sant'Angelo.

Lara absently stroked Hero and she lay down at her feet, curling up trustingly. She said to Ciro, 'Thank you for letting me keep her.'

Ciro shrugged, and then he looked at his watch. 'You wanted to visit the Guggenheim Museum, didn't you?'

Lara nodded, surprised he'd remembered her saying that the other night at a function.

'I can take the afternoon off—we'll go after lunch.'

Lara felt a dangerous fluttering in her belly

and said, 'Oh, it's okay…you don't have to. I can go by myself—'

'Don't you want me to come with you?'

Lara could feel her face grow hot. This teasing, relaxed Ciro was so reminiscent of how he'd been before that it was painful. 'Of course I'd love to see it with you.'

Ciro stood up. '*Va bene.* I've a few calls to make—we'll leave in an hour.'

Lara watched him leave, striding off the terrace back into the house. She took a deep breath—anything to try and get oxygen to her brain and keep herself from imagining impossible things.

Like the fact that Ciro might actually be learning to like her again…

The following day Ciro watched Lara play on the lawn with the puppy from the window in his study. She was wearing shorts and her long slim legs had taken on a light golden glow. She wore a silk cropped top and he could see tantalising slivers of her belly when it rode up as she moved.

He might have cursed her for trying to tempt

him, but he knew she wasn't even aware that he'd come home early. *Home early.* Since when had he started to come home early? Or work from home? Or take afternoons off to go to a museum? The only person who'd ever had that effect on him was on her back, laughing as the puppy climbed all over her, yapping excitedly.

There was a bone-deep sense of satisfaction in his body from night after night of mind-blowing sex. He'd stopped sending Lara back to her own bed. She effectively shared his room now—something he'd never done with another woman, far too wary of inviting an intimacy that would be misread, or taken advantage of.

And they'd spent hours wandering around the Guggenheim the day before. It had been one of the most pleasant afternoons Ciro could remember in a long time.

As he looked at Lara now he had to acknowledge that his desire for her wasn't waning. Far from it. It seemed to be intensifying. But if he stuck to his agreement with her they'd be divorcing—at the earliest in only a few months. That thought sent something not unlike panic into his gut.

So far she'd fulfilled her side of the marriage, and introduced him to people who would never have welcomed him into their sphere before. He had a list of new deals to consider. Invitations to events and places he'd never been allowed access to before. All because of her.

But in truth, he found it hard to focus on that when she filled his vision and he spent most days reliving the night before and anticipating the night ahead.

She was not what he'd expected. More like the Lara he'd known first. And if this was an elaborate act, then what was the point? He couldn't figure it out, but something wasn't matching up…

At that moment his phone rang and he answered it impatiently, only half listening as he watched Lara throwing a ball for the puppy.

He turned away from the view, though, after his solicitor had finished speaking. 'Repeat what you just said.'

'I said that we know who was behind the kidnapping, Ciro, and I don't think you're going to like what you hear.'

* * *

The sun was throwing long shadows on the grass by the time Lara picked up Hero and went back inside the house. All was quiet except for the dull hum of Manhattan traffic outside.

But then she heard a sound coming from the main reception room, and put Hero down in her bed before investigating. She walked in to find Ciro throwing back a shot of alcohol. Predictably, her heart rate increased.

'I didn't know you were home.'

Her heart fluttered at the thought that maybe he'd come back early to take her on another excursion. But when he turned around she had to stifle a gasp. He was pale, and she realised he was pale with fury, because his eyes were burning.

'What is it? What's wrong?'

Ciro put the empty glass back on the tray with exaggerated care and then he looked back at Lara. She had only the faintest prickling sense of foreboding before he said, 'So, when were you going to tell me that you and your uncle were behind the kidnap plot?'

Lara's insides turned to ice. 'How do you know about that?'

'I've been investigating the kidnap since it happened. I kept hitting dead ends until now. Is it true?'

Lara felt sick. She nodded her head slowly.

Not exactly, but... 'Yes. My uncle planned it. He didn't want us to marry.'

Ciro's lip curled. 'And so he came up with a lurid plan to have us kidnapped? Or was that your contribution?'

Lara shook her head. She felt as if she was drowning, and moved sluggishly over to a chair where she sat down. 'I didn't know anything about it...not until after.'

Ciro looked at Lara. He couldn't believe it. Couldn't believe that after everything he'd been through with this woman she had done it again. The emotion he felt transcended anger. He was icy cold with it. Far worse than heat and rage.

He could feel the livid line of his scar. The phantom throbbing of his little finger. He wanted to go over and haul Lara up to stand. She looked pathetically, unbelievably shocked.

'I want to know everything. *Now.*'

He saw her swallow. She was so pale he almost felt the sting of his conscience but he ruthlessly pushed it down. This woman was the worst kind of chameleon. And potentially a criminal.

'I was forced to marry Henry Winterborne. By my uncle.'

Ciro shook his head. 'That's ridiculous.'

'I wish it was. My uncle was obsessed with status and lineage. There was no way he was going to allow me to marry you. But it went much further than that.'

Ciro said nothing. He saw Lara clasp her hands together and in that moment had a flashback to how her hands had felt on his buttocks only hours before, squeezing him, huskily begging him for more.

He gritted out, 'Keep going.'

'My uncle was in debt. Serious debt. Millions and millions of pounds. He'd run through his fortune—and my trust fund. I was his only hope of saving his reputation and clearing the debt. He'd had us followed from the moment I mentioned you to him. He knew we were serious.'

Ciro said nothing so Lara continued.

'He knew that I was sheltered…not experienced. He was fairly certain we hadn't…'

Remarkably, colour stained her cheeks, and it made Ciro feel so many conflicting things that he decided to focus on the anger.

'Save your blushes, *cara*. This really is the most intriguing story.'

Lara's mouth tightened for a moment, but then she said, 'He sold me—like a slave girl at an auction. To Henry Winterborne, the highest bidder.'

Ciro struggled to take this in. It was such a far-fetched story. He decided to see how far Lara would go towards hanging herself and pretending she was an innocent player. 'When are you claiming that you knew about this?'

'I didn't know until after the kidnapping. That's when he told me. And that's when he told me he would kill you if I pursued the relationship.'

'So you came to the hospital to convince me you'd never wanted to marry me in order to *save* me? *Cara*, that is the most romantic thing I've heard in my whole life.'

Something occurred to Ciro then, and he went very still.

Then he said, 'I told you that story in Sicily... about my great-grandmother. About how she couldn't marry the man she wanted, how he was threatened. You appropriated it as your own... You didn't even have the creativity to come up with something original. You make me—'

Lara shot up from the chair. 'It's true—I swear. That's just a coincidence. It all happened exactly like I said.'

Ciro forced down his anger. Forced himself to stay civil just for a little longer. 'So why didn't you tell me this when you had the chance at the hospital? We were alone—no one to hear you tell me the gory details.'

He held up his hand when she opened her mouth.

'I'll tell you why, shall I? Because even though you might not have liked the idea of marrying an old man, it was still preferable to marrying a man of no lineage except a dubious one, hmm?'

She shook her head. 'No. I would never have

wanted to marry that man—not in a million years. He disgusted me.'

'So why didn't you leave him? He was in a wheelchair—he could hardly run after you.'

He saw Lara flinch minutely at that and he crushed the spark of emotion when he thought of her being threatened. For all he knew that was an elaborate fabrication.

'My uncle was alive until three months before Henry Winterborne died. The whole time he held the threat of doing you harm over my head. I had nothing—no money and nowhere to go. I felt guilty because I had put Henry in a wheelchair. And then, after he had the stroke, it was clear he was dying, so I felt even less able to try and leave.'

Ciro snorted. 'No money? The man was a millionaire.'

Lara avoided his eye. 'After the accident…he was angry. He gave me nothing.'

Ciro's fury increased—she was manipulating him again with this wildly elaborate tale. He wasn't even sure to what end, but he felt sure it couldn't be as simple as she was making out. And he'd had enough.

Ciro's voice was low and lethal. 'I don't know why you're doing this, Lara, but it serves no purpose.'

Lara could see the total rejection of what she'd said on Ciro's face…hear it in his voice. It was exactly as she'd feared. Worse. She could also see the torment of those dark memories in the lines etched into his face.

She'd witnessed his horrific nightmares. Instinctively she reached out towards him. 'Ciro, I'm so sorry. I never meant for any of this to happen—'

He lifted his hand to stop her words. '*Basta.* Enough. My investigative team haven't ruled out your involvement with your uncle. You *do* know you could be prosecuted for this?'

She went pale again—white as parchment. 'Ciro, please, you have to listen to me… I knew nothing. I was as much a victim as you were. I loved you so much… I was terrified of what my uncle might do. I had no choice.'

Ciro's expression turned to one of disgust. 'You *loved* me? You go too far, Lara.' He continued, 'If what you say is true—and I'll verify that myself—how do you explain not telling me all this when we met again?'

She swallowed. 'I was afraid you wouldn't believe me—and apparently I was right.'

Ciro's expression got even darker. 'Not good enough. The truth is that you colluded with your uncle in sending me a message to stay away from you. You could have just *told* me you didn't want to marry me—you didn't have to go to such dramatic lengths.'

Lara realised that further defence would be futile. She said, 'Do you remember I asked you if you loved me, that day in the hospital?'

A flash of irritation crossed Ciro's face. 'What does that have to do with anything?'

'I did want to tell you everything. In spite of my uncle's threats...in spite of the kidnapping... I believed that somehow you'd be able to fight him. But when I knew you didn't feel the same for me as I felt for you, I believed there was no point in risking your life.'

He looked at her for such a long moment that Lara almost believed for a second that she might have got through—but then he said in a toneless voice, 'I've heard enough, Lara. Enough to last a lifetime. This marriage is over—we're done. I want you to leave today. Right now. I'll organise getting you on a flight back to the UK. If you leave with no fuss I'll consider not pressing charges. To be perfectly frank you're not worth the legal hassle or the headlines. Now, get out of my sight.'

A numbness was spreading from Lara's heart outwards to every extremity. She moved jerkily away from Ciro, towards the door. When she got there she stopped and turned around. Ciro was staring at her with such disgust on his face that she almost balked.

She grabbed the door knob to try and stay standing. 'I love you, Ciro. I always have. I did what I thought was best for you and it almost killed me. The last two years have been purgatory. I won't apologise for loving you, whether you choose to believe me or not. And I'm sorry I had to lie to you.'

She left then, before he could say anything caustic. He didn't love her. He'd never loved her, and this was the final lethal blow.

It all happened with military precision. Staff came and helped her to pack, but she insisted on taking just a small case with the belongings she'd arrived with. A car was waiting to take her to JFK, and she was on-board a flight within a few hours.

She'd had to leave Hero behind, as the dog didn't have documentation, and Lara hadn't seen Ciro before she left, so she wasn't even sure he'd still been there. But one thing was certain. She'd never see him again.

The following evening Ciro sat in the back of his car as it inched its way down Fifth Avenue towards Central Park and his house. His heart was beating a little too fast and he had to modulate his breathing. It was at times like this that he felt most claustrophobic—when he cursed the kidnappers for doing what they had to him, so that no matter how strong he was mentally he still felt a residue of fear that clung to him like a toxic tentacle whenever he was in a small confined space.

He hated it that he couldn't just ease his sense of claustrophobia by jumping out of the car to walk, because he'd spark a massive security alert.

The thought occurred to him that when Lara had been in the back of the car with him he hadn't noticed the claustrophobia as much. He'd been too distracted by her. He scowled at that.

Since the revelations of yesterday, and Lara's departure, he'd been existing in a kind of fog. He couldn't recollect what he'd done today, exactly. The puppy had barked pitifully that morning and Ciro had let her out into the garden, where she'd sniffed around disconsolately in between directing accusatory looks his way.

For a man who was used to thinking clearly he was beyond irritated that he was still thinking of her.

Whether or not it was true that she hadn't colluded with her uncle, she'd *known* about the kidnapping the day she'd come to him at the hospital. He would never forget the blasé way she'd dropped her bombshell that day. When he'd been lying there, beaten and battered. *Because of her!* She'd had her chance and she'd said nothing.

Last night had been the first night he'd spent alone in his bed in weeks. He'd had the nightmare again—except this time he hadn't woken to the cooling touch of Lara's hand or her tempting body. He'd woken sweating, tangled in the sheets, his voice hoarse from shouting. And this time the dream had been slightly different—it had been one moment, repeated over and over. The moment they'd ripped Lara out of his arms and opened the van door to dump her outside.

Her voice drifted into his head then: *'Do you remember I asked you if you loved me?'* He did, actually. He shifted in his seat now, feeling uncomfortable. He did recall it, and he also recalled the feeling of panic that had gripped him.

Love.

He remembered thinking of his father and his slavish devotion to his unfaithful wife, how it had disgusted him. If that was love then, no, he didn't feel that. But there had been something almost desperate on Lara's face and so he'd made some platitude.

What about the terror you felt when she was taken from you by the kidnappers? In that moment you thought you loved her.

Ciro shifted uncomfortably again. He'd always put that surge of emotion down to the extreme circumstances.

His staff had informed him that her flight had left on time yesterday. She'd be back in the UK now. She could be anywhere. For the first time in two years he didn't have tabs on her.

Before the car had even come to a standstill outside his house Ciro got out, not liking the panicky feeling in his gut. He went inside, dropping his things, and the puppy sped across the tiled floor towards him, yapping. It was quickly followed by the housekeeper, apologising profusely. Ciro picked Hero up and waved away the apology.

Feeling restless, he climbed the stairs to the bedrooms. He stood outside Lara's door for a long moment, and then an image of his father came into his head and he scowled and pushed the door open.

It had been tidied, and the bed remade. It was as if she'd never been there. But he could still smell her scent in the air. Lemon and roses.

He put the puppy down on the bed, where she promptly curled up and went to sleep.

Ciro went to the dressing room and opened

the doors, expecting to find it empty. But it was full of clothes. He frowned. Everything he'd bought her was there. As was her jewellery. Neatly lined up on velvet pouches under glass display cases.

He went and picked up the phone in the room and rang down to the housekeeper. 'What did Lar— Mrs Sant'Angelo take with her when she left?'

He listened for a moment and then hung up, sitting down on the bed. She'd taken one suitcase. And he knew which one. The one she'd come with. The battered one.

The puppy crept towards him and got into his lap. Ciro stroked her absently. After a while he stood up, taking her with him. He left her with the housekeeper in the kitchen.

Still feeling restless, Ciro went into the reception room. It was filled with priceless paintings and *objets d'art*... Persian rugs. It could be a museum it was so still and stuffy.

When he'd bought this property he'd felt as if he'd reached a pinnacle. One of the many he'd set himself. Then, when he'd proposed to Lara, he'd imagined her here as his wife and hostess.

Charming people with her natural warmth and compassion.

Giving you access to a higher level of society, reminded a voice.

A crystal decanter glinted at him from the drinks tray nearby. It seemed to mock him for thinking he'd had it all worked out. For believing that he'd had his fill of Lara. That he was done with her. For believing that all this excess around him actually meant anything.

The tightness in Ciro's chest intensified, and with an inarticulate surge of rage he grabbed the decanter and threw it at the massive stone fireplace, where it smashed into a million pieces.

He heard footsteps running, and for some inexplicable reason he thought it might be—

But when he turned around it was just a shocked-looking staff member.

'Is everything okay, Mr Sant'Angelo?'

He felt ragged. Undone. Empty.

'Everything is fine.'

But he knew it wasn't.

'Two pints of bitter, love!'

Lara forced a smile. 'Coming up.'

After-work drinks on a warm Indian summer evening in London meant packed pubs with people spilling out onto the pavements. Laughing, joking. Delighted that the end of the week had come and they had two days off stretching ahead.

Lara didn't have two days off. At weekends she worked in a small Italian restaurant, near where she was living at a hostel in Kentish Town. But she refused to feel sorry for herself as she went outside with the two pints and collected money and dirty glasses.

A man leaned towards her. 'You're far too pretty to be working here, love. Let me take you out of this cesspit and we'll run away.'

His friends guffawed loudly, but ridiculously Lara couldn't even force a fake laugh. She felt tears sting her eyes. Which was pathetic. She was lucky to have found two jobs. She was earning her own money for the first time in her life. She was finally free… If only that freedom didn't feel so heavy.

She never thought about…*him*. She couldn't. Not if she wanted to keep it together.

'Hey, gorgeous! A pint and a white wine, please!'

Lara looked up at the flushed face of a city boy and forced herself to smile. 'Coming up.'

CHAPTER NINE

A WEEK LATER Ciro was back in London. He was at a black tie event in Buckingham Palace. Lesser members of the royal family mingled with the guests, and he'd just had a long conversation with a man who was in direct line to the throne of England. And it hadn't just been an idle conversation—it had been about business. Ciro's business.

He looked around. This was literally the inner sanctum—the most exclusive group of people on the planet. And he, Ciro Sant'Angelo, a man descended from pirates and Mafiosi, was standing among them. Accepted. Respected. *Finally.*

So why wasn't he feeling more satisfied?

Because he'd just had a call from his solicitor to say that Lara had finally been in touch about going forward with divorce proceedings and had given him a PO box address. She'd told his solicitor that she had no interest in taking the money due to her in the event of their divorce and had named a charity for it to be sent to, if they insisted.

Ciro's charity—Face Forward.

And other things had come to light too—discomfiting things. He'd found the credit card he'd given her on the desk in his study in New York. And her engagement ring and wedding ring, which were both worth a small fortune.

There had been a note.

I'll pay back what I owe.

On inspection, there had been a sum of just a few hundred dollars owing on the card. A laughable amount to someone like Ciro.

She'd also said that once Hero had her papers in order she would appreciate being reunited with the dog. And a parcel had arrived for her. When Ciro had opened it, it had contained a wedding dress. Clearly from the eighties. It wasn't even new.

Nothing made sense.

He had to acknowledge uncomfortably that the Lara who had appeared in his hospital room that day…the unrecognisable Lara…he'd never seen her again. Just flashes at the beginning. If she really was some rich bitch who had only been concerned with status and wealth, then wouldn't she have fleeced him for all he was worth?

Wouldn't she be here right now? Her elegant blonde head shining like a jewel amongst the dross, dressed in a silky evening gown as she hunted for a new husband?

A feeling of clammy desperation stole over Ciro. Maybe she was still playing him. Maybe she *was* here. He looked around, heart thumping, almost expecting to see her blonde head, hear her low, seductive laugh…

'Who are you looking for, Sant'Angelo? Your wife? Have you mislaid her?'

Ciro looked to his right and down into the florid features of a man whose name he'd forgotten and whom he had never liked on previous acquaintance.

'No,' he said tightly. 'She's not here.'

Where the hell is she?

'Pity,' said the man, leaning in a little. 'She's a rare jewel. But I doubt she's *that* rare any more…' He winked. 'If you get what I mean…

After all, she's been married twice now. Winterborne got the best of her, lucky sod. If I'd had more money at the time maybe it would have been me.'

Ciro looked at the man with an awful kind of cold horror sinking into his blood. 'What on earth are you talking about?'

The man looked up at him and suddenly appeared uncomfortable. 'Ah… I thought you knew… The auction, of course. I mean, obviously it wasn't a *real* auction. Just something between a few of Thomas Templeton's friends. Girls like Lara are few and far between these days. Innocent. Pure…'

Lara's voice was in Ciro's head. *'He sold me like a slave girl at an auction. To Henry Winterborne, the highest bidder.'*

The man slapped him on the shoulder. 'All right there, Sant'Angelo? You've gone very pale.'

Ciro felt sick to his stomach. 'How many men were involved?' he managed to get out.

Blissfully unaware of the volcano building inside Ciro, the man looked around and said conspiratorially, 'There's always a market for girls like her. With the right breeding. Especially virgins. It's a rare commodity these days, you know.'

Ciro didn't stop to think. His right hand swung back and his fist connected with the fleshy part of the man's face, sending him windmilling backwards into the crowd, where he collided with a waiter holding a tray of glasses, and a woman, who shrieked just before he landed in a heavy heap on the ground.

Instantly security men were beside Ciro, taking his arms in their hands. He briefly caught the eye of the member of the royal family he'd been talking to and saw disdain spreading over his aristocratic features. Everyone was staring at him. Shocked. And then they started whispering as Ciro was led out.

And he didn't give a damn.

For the first time in his life, he didn't give a damn.

It was another hot, muggy evening in the bar and Lara's feet were aching. But at least she wasn't wearing heels any more. She was wiping down the counter under the bar when she heard it.

'Lara.'

She stopped. She'd dreamed about him nearly every night. Was she hallucinating now?

She kept cleaning.

'Lara.'

She looked up and her heart jumped into her throat. *Ciro.* Standing head and shoulders above everyone else around him at the bar.

'Oi, mate—if you're going to take up space at the bar, put in an order for us too, will ya?'

A group of young guys behind Ciro sniggered. He ignored them.

Lara gripped the cloth. 'What are you doing here?'

'Can we talk?'

She noticed that he looked drawn. Dishevelled. 'Is something wrong? Has something happened?'

He shook his head. 'Everything is fine...but we need to talk.'

It was the familiar bossy tone that reassured her in the end—and also told her that this was real, not a fantasy. She was aware of her grumpy boss hovering…aware that no drinks were being served.

Lara sent her boss a reassuring glance and said to Ciro, 'I can't just leave. Sit down and I'll bring you a beer. You'll have to wait until my shift ends.'

'How long is that?'

'Three hours.'

She ignored his look of affront and handed him a pint of bitter, willing him to disappear. Eventually he turned away when she started serving the people behind him.

It was the most excruciating three hours Lara had experienced. With every move she made she was aware of Ciro's eyes burning into her from where he was sitting in a corner. She was surprised she didn't drop every glass, fumble every order.

But finally the pub was empty and she stood in front of Ciro in beer-spattered jeans and T-shirt, a cardigan over her arm and her bag across her body. She felt exhausted, but also energised.

'Where do you want to talk?'

Ciro stood up. 'Do you live near here?'

Lara walked with him out of the pub. She saw Ciro's security team nearby, and his car and driver. She thought of the hostel she called home.

'I don't think you'd like where I'm living. There's a late-night café near here that should still be open.'

'We could go to the townhouse.'

Lara immediately shook her head. *That* London was a million miles from her life now. 'No.'

'Fine—where's this café?'

Lara led him around the corner and into the friendly café. They were given a booth at the back. Ciro commanded attention and special treatment even here.

Lara ordered tea; Ciro coffee.

When the drinks were delivered, Lara said, 'So what do you want to talk about?'

For a second Ciro looked comically nonplussed, and then he said, 'You left no forwarding address.'

Lara stifled the hurt of recalling that moment in New York. 'You kicked me out, Ciro. I didn't think my forwarding address was high on your list of priorities. I contacted your solicitor with my details.'

'A PO box. What even *is* that?'

Anger surged. If he'd just come here to harangue her because she wasn't following divorce etiquette properly... 'I'm living in a hostel, Ciro. I don't know where I'll be in a month's time. That's why I have a PO box.'

Now he looked horrified. 'A *hostel*?'

Lara nodded. 'It's perfectly clean and habitable.'

Ciro had gone pale under his tan. Lara refused to let it move her.

He put a parcel on the table and said, 'This arrived for you. I opened it. Why did you buy a wedding dress, Lara?'

Lara pulled the package towards her, lifting out the familiar dress. Her mother's wedding dress. She'd tracked it down online and it had only been a couple of hundred dollars to buy it back. Emotion surged in her chest. *She had it back*.

She fought to keep her composure. 'It was my mother's wedding dress. I sold it once.' Tears blurred her vision but she blinked them away, saying as briskly as she could, 'Thank you. I'll pay you back.'

'Why did you sell your mother's dress in the first place?'

Lara avoided looking at him in case he saw how much this dress meant to her. When she felt composed enough, she looked at Ciro. 'I needed the money. After Henry Winterborne got injured I was useless to him. He made me work for him—for free, of course. He sacked his housekeeper. I put up with it because my uncle was still alive and he continued to hold the threat of hurting you over my head. I think he was scared I'd go to you, ask for help. Or that I'd try to warn you. I fantasised about doing that so many times.' Lara touched the package. 'I'd hoped to wear this dress when I married you...it was a connection to my mother. A piece of the past.'

'But you sold it?'

Lara looked at him again. 'The housekeeper who had worked for Henry Winterborne...we'd become friendly. After losing her job she was in dire straits. Her husband had lost his job and was ill... She couldn't find work. I couldn't do much, but I sold this dress and some of my other clothes. Some jewellery. I tried to help her. I felt responsible.'

'Why on earth did you feel responsible?'

Ciro sounded almost angry. Lara avoided his eye. 'If I hadn't injured Henry Winterborne—'

Ciro cut her off. '*Dio*, Lara. The man would have raped you if he could. It wasn't your fault.'

Lara felt a flutter in her chest. *Dangerous*. She looked at Ciro. 'Why are you here?'

'You don't want anything? From the divorce?'

She shook her head, stifling the disappointment. He'd only tracked her down because he needed to discuss this. He probably didn't believe her.

'It was never about money for me. Ever. Not the first time around. Not now.'

Ciro pulled out a tabloid newspaper and handed it to Lara. He said, 'I presume you haven't seen this?'

She looked down and gasped. On the front page there was a picture of Ciro in handcuffs, being put into a police car. His knuckles were bleeding and he looked grimmer than she'd ever seen him. The headline read: *Sant'Angelo Brawls in Palace Amongst Royalty!*

She took in the few words underneath.

You can take the man out of the Mafia...

Lara looked at him, shocked. 'What happened?'

Ciro said, 'I met a man. He was one of the men at the select little auction run by your uncle. One of the men who—' He stopped.

Lara finished for him, feeling sick. 'One of the men who might have become my husband?'

Ciro nodded.

He flexed his hand and Lara reached for it, turning it over to see his bruised knuckles. She said quietly, 'Thank you, but you didn't have to do that. You must hate the press attention.'

Ciro flipped his hand so he held hers. 'I don't care about any of that. Finally I've got it through my thick skull that it doesn't matter. Respect and acceptance come from living with integrity and honesty. I can't do more than that and I'm done trying.'

Lara was almost too scared to breathe for a moment. She looked at Ciro and saw a blazing light in his eyes. Something she'd never seen before. A different kind of pride. It made her emotions bubble up again.

'You've never needed to. You tower above men like my uncle and Henry Winterborne. You always have. But I can understand your father and his father's desire for acceptance. They deserved better.'

Ciro huffed a laugh. He still held Lara's hand. 'Did they? They had blood on their hands, Lara. We all did, by association—although we've come a long way since those times. I'll never be fully accepted into that world, but what I've realised is that money and commerce talk more than social acceptance. That's all that matters in growing a business and a reputation.'

His scar stood out against his olive skin and Lara's emotions finally got the better of her. Ciro would never have had to come to this painful realisation if not for her.

'I'm so sorry, Ciro. If we hadn't met…if I hadn't fallen in love with you…my uncle never would have—' She stopped, biting her lip to stem the tears threatening to flow down her cheeks.

His grip on her hand tightened. 'You have nothing to be sorry for, Lara. *Nothing.* From the moment we met again you confounded me. I expected the woman who had appeared in my hospital room that day, but I got *you*. The Lara I remembered. Except I couldn't trust it. You. I was afraid to after you hurt me so badly.'

Lara chest seized. '*Hurt...?* But you didn't have any feelings for me.'

Ciro huffed out a sound halfway between a laugh and a groan, his hand still tight on hers. 'I didn't know *what* I was feeling. All I knew was that when you asked me if I loved you I panicked. All I could think of was my father, and his toxic obsessive love of my mother. I knew it wasn't that I felt. But I couldn't deny that I felt obsessive about you, and suddenly I was terrified that I was just like my father—that I would lose myself over a woman and make a fool of myself like he had.'

Before Lara could fully absorb this, or what it meant, Ciro asked her a question.

'Why did you agree to marry me this time?'

She swallowed her emotions. 'I felt so guilty

for what had happened to you. I owed you. After everything that had happened…'

Ciro took his hand from hers, his expression changing. 'You felt obliged…' He grimaced. 'And why wouldn't you? I *told* you that you owed me.'

He looked at her and she saw pain in his eyes. The pride was gone.

'You had nowhere to go. No money. You felt guilty already. I left you no choice.'

Lara shook her head. 'Of course I had a choice. I could have walked away… I could have told you everything that day and let the chips fall where they may. But I didn't.'

'Why didn't you?'

She kept looking at him, even though it was hard. 'Because you were back in my life. I didn't tell you because I'd convinced myself I owed it to you. I was afraid that if I told you everything you'd despise me even more than you already did.' She took a deep breath. 'Even though I denied it to myself I still loved you, I would have done anything to be with you— even let you take your revenge out on me.'

Ciro looked shell-shocked. 'What you went

through…for two years… When I think of that man and what he could have done to you if you hadn't been brave enough to fight him off…'
He stood up abruptly and stalked out of the café.

Shocked, Lara sat there for a moment, before throwing down some cash and grabbing the wedding dress. He was outside on the empty street, a fist up to his mouth. When she got close he turned away from her, but not before she'd seen the agony on his face. Moisture on his cheeks.

'Ciro—'

His voice was thick. 'Don't look at me. I can't bear it, Lara. To know what you went through because I was too much of a coward to own up to my feelings…'

Lara went and hugged him from behind, resting her head against his back. The parcel fell by her feet, unnoticed.

Eventually he turned around and she sucked in a breath at the ravaged look on his face.

'How can you ever forgive me?'

A weight lodged in her gut. She'd never expected to see this: Ciro feeling guilty. *She* was the guilty one.

She reached up and wiped away the moisture on his face, her heart aching, because she knew that even though Ciro might have feelings for her it wasn't love, and she would have to walk away again.

'It was my fault—' she said.

He shook his head. '*No*. Never say that again. It was your uncle. Lara, I've had him investigated. You have no idea how corrupt he was. What he did to you was the tip of the iceberg. He was involved in fraud, and in trafficking women in and out of the UK.'

Lara's hands dropped. 'My God…'

'Lara… I'm so sorry.'

She was unable to speak. She'd never expected the cruel irony of Ciro feeling guilty. Saying sorry.

He took her hand. 'This isn't a conversation for here. Come with me to the townhouse— please?'

Lara knew that she should pull back. She'd heard all she needed to. Ciro was right. It wasn't her fault. Or his. They'd both been used as pawns. But she couldn't pull away—not just yet. Soon she'd have a lifetime to try and forget him.

'Okay.'

Ciro picked up the wedding dress and led her over to his car, where she got into the back. When he got in on the other side, he surprised her by pulling her into his arms, enfolding her close. She closed her eyes and guiltily revelled in his strength. It wouldn't last. He just felt guilty. But she'd take it while she could.

Amazingly, she fell asleep, with Ciro's heartbeat thudding against her cheek. She was only vaguely aware of the car stopping, of Ciro lifting her out and carrying her. There was another familiar voice. And then she was being put down on a soft surface and a warm blanket was being pulled over her.

She struggled to wake up but Ciro's commanding voice said, 'No, go to sleep, Lara. You need to rest.'

When Lara woke the next morning it was early. Just after dawn. It took a minute for her to realise that she wasn't in her disinfectant-scented room at the hostel. She was in a luxurious bed.

Ciro's townhouse.

She sat up and looked down, grimacing. She was still dressed in her T-shirt and jeans. A faint smell of beer and fried food wafted up. She got up and went into the bathroom, stripping off and stepping under the shower.

As the water sluiced down over her body she finally allowed herself to remember the previous cataclysmic evening. The outpouring of emotion. The pain on Ciro's face.

The fact that he didn't love her but that he was sorry.

Lara hugged herself under the water for a long moment, willing back the emotion. She had to hold it in until she left this place. Then she could grieve. *Finally.*

When Lara stepped out of the shower she felt lighter, in spite of the heaviness in her heart. Cleansed. At peace. She had something she could hold to her and cherish, no matter what happened with Ciro.

Because, in spite of the catharsis of the truth finally being revealed, and what he'd said about his priorities, she knew him too well. She knew he would have had time now to assess what had happened, and that he must be mortified by how much he'd revealed. Not to mention the public humiliation of being arrested at a party in Buckingham Palace.

He wouldn't thank her for that when he realised the full extent of the repercussions. He'd worked too hard not to mind.

She pulled on a towelling robe from the back of the door and made her way downstairs to the utility room with her clothes, intending to wash and dry them.

When she was on her way back up she heard a noise in the kitchen and went in. Ciro was there, in jeans and a shirt, sipping a cup of coffee. He turned to face her and she felt shy. Ridiculously.

'I'm sorry about that—falling asleep. I must have been more tired than I thought.'

Ciro looked stern. 'I'm not surprised…working two jobs.'

Lara's mouth fell open. 'How did you know?'

'I tracked you down a few days ago. My investigators told me.'

Lara tried not to sound defensive. 'I need the money.'

Ciro changed the subject. 'Coffee?'

Lara nodded. 'Please.'

She tried to gauge his mood but it was hard. He wasn't exhibiting any sign of the emotion of last night and her worst fears seemed to be coming true. He was regretting having said anything.

He handed her a cup. 'Let's talk upstairs.'

'We really don't have to. You must be busy. And I have to get to work at the restaurant—'

He stopped her. 'You're not working there again.'

'Ciro, I can't just—'

'Come upstairs with me. Please.'

Lara followed him, trying not to give in to the anger and panic that Ciro was riding roughshod over her life all over again.

He led her into one of the informal living rooms, with soft slouchy sofas and chairs. She took a chair and Ciro walked to the window. She tried not to let her gaze drop to where the material of his snug jeans hugged his buttocks so lovingly.

She took a fortifying sip of coffee and put down her cup. 'As soon as my clothes are dry I'll get out of your hair. I know you mean well, but I really can't afford to lose that job—'

Ciro whirled around, the first crack in his calm façade showing. 'I said you are *not* going back there, Lara. *Dio.*' He put down his own cup and shoved his hands deep in his jeans pockets, as if afraid he might do something bad with them.

Lara was stunned into silence. She saw a muscle beating in his jaw.

'This house is your house, Lara. You have somewhere to live. You don't need to work to put a roof over your head. Ever again.'

She looked at him. Totally confused. 'You're giving me your house?'

'I mean, it's *ours*. My home is your home.'

She shook her head. 'I don't… What are you saying, Ciro?'

He came over and sat down. Stood up. Sat down again. Suddenly she could see the emotion on his face.

'I'm saying that I want us to stay married, Lara. But after everything you've been through… I know you deserve your independence. You've had people—*men*—telling you what to do since you lost your family, and I don't want to just be another man running your life.'

Lara's heart constricted. 'You don't want me to go?'

He shook his head, kneeling down beside her. '*No*. I *don't* want you to leave. *Ever*. But I also don't want you to feel obliged to stay because you feel like you owe me, or because of guilt. I love you, Lara, but I don't want you to feel trapped.'

The world stopped on its axis. 'You…what?'

Ciro frowned. 'I love you… I told you yesterday…'

Lara shook her head. 'No. I'm pretty sure I would have remembered that piece of information. You were upset…feeling guilty… You mentioned *feelings*. But you never mentioned love.'

Ciro took her hand. 'Well, I do love you. I've loved you since the moment I laid eyes on you in that street in Florence. I just didn't know what it was. You were the first woman to get under my skin without even trying, Lara. The first woman I spent a whole night with in my bed. When I proposed to you it was because you were the first woman who made me want more. Who made me hate the cynicism I'd been brought up with.'

Ciro went pale.

'When those kidnappers ripped you out of my arms that day...that's when I knew... But even afterwards I told myself that it couldn't be *love*. I would never be so foolish, such a slave to my emotions—not like my father.'

Lara saw it on his face. Pure emotion. She put a hand to her mouth to stifle a sound of pure joy mixed with shock.

But Ciro took her hand down. 'Please believe me, Lara. I love you more than life itself. Without you the world didn't make sense. I never truly believed you were that person you'd turned into in the hospital, but it was easier to believe that than admit you'd broken my heart.'

Lara touched his face, his scar. Tears blurred her vision. 'Oh, my love...my darling. I'm so sorry.'

He caught her face in his hands. He looked fierce. 'Never say sorry again. *Never.*'

She nodded. 'I love you...so much.'

Ciro shook his head. 'I'm almost scared to believe... We've been through so much—I've put you through so much...'

Lara put a finger to his mouth, stopping his words. 'Don't *you* ever say that again. Neither of us were to blame. We got caught up in events outside our control. I love you, my darling, and that's all you have to believe.'

She bent forward and kissed him. A sweet chaste kiss. Then she pulled back and said shakily, 'Even if you had told me you loved me, and we'd stood up to my uncle, I dread to think what might have happened. He was crazy, Ciro. I was his only hope of redemption and he was capable of anything.'

Ciro was grim. 'Maybe—but he put us through two years of hell.' He said then, 'Do you know why I really bought this house?'

She shook her head, marvelling at how full her heart could feel.

'I kept tabs on you for those two years...hoping for God knows what to happen. I knew where you lived and I bought this house sight unseen. I think I had nefarious plans to seduce you away from Henry Winterborne. It would have proved that you had no morals, but more importantly it would have brought you back to me. I had no qualms about playing dirty to get you back.'

Lara smiled a shaky smile. 'You have no idea how many nights I dreamed of you coming to rescue me. But then I'd see photos of you, out and about, getting on with your life, with other women...'

The pain of that still made her gut churn. She looked away.

Ciro caught her chin and turned her back to face him. 'I didn't take one of those women into my bed. I couldn't. The thought of you—it consumed me. You ruined me for anyone else. *Ever.*'

Lara couldn't hold back. She flung her arms around Ciro and he caught her. Lifted her up and sat down on the sofa, settling her across his lap. Cradling her.

Lara clutched at his shirt. 'We've wasted so much time...'

He caught her chin again, tipping it up. 'No. We start again now. No more regrets, okay?'

Lara nodded, humbled by Ciro's capacity to forgive and move on.

He sat up then, and put her beside him. Then he got off the sofa and down on one knee in front of her.

'Ciro...'

He drew a box out of his jeans pocket. A familiar velvet box. Her heart tripped. He opened it and she saw her engagement ring and wedding ring.

Ciro suddenly looked anxious. 'Maybe I should have bought new ones.'

Lara touched them reverently. 'No, I love them.'

He took the rings out of the box and looked at her. 'Lara Sant'Angelo, will you please stay my wife—for the rest of our lives?'

She nodded, and got out a choked, 'Yes.'

When the rings were back on her finger, where they belonged, she said, 'I wondered why you hadn't thrown the engagement ring away...'

Ciro looked deep into her eyes and said huskily, 'Maybe because I was already dreaming of this moment.'

He kissed her then, so deeply that he touched her heart and mended all the broken shards back together.

Much later, when they were lying in bed, sated and at peace, Lara said, 'I think maybe that's why I tracked down my mother's wedding dress when I had the chance. Maybe I was hoping for a second chance.'

Ciro caught her hand and her rings sparkled. He kissed her there and she looked at him, caught in those dark eyes that held so much love.

'Second chances and new beginnings.'

'Yes, my love, for ever.'

EPILOGUE

A month later...

Dusk was melting into night as Lara walked to the entrance of the small chapel in the grounds of the *palazzo* in Sicily. Apparently it was a tradition, marrying at night. She didn't really care.

Lighted torches had guided her from the *palazzo* to the chapel and to Isabella, who was her bridesmaid. The young girl's eyes were suspiciously shiny as she fussed over Lara at the entrance, where flowers festooned the doorway, making the air heavy with a million scents.

Hero danced around their feet, looking up at Lara adoringly. She was attached to Isabella's wrist with a ribbon and had a velvet cushion tied to her collar, upon which was tied a gold wedding band inlaid with sapphires. A new wedding ring to celebrate this renewal of their vows.

'Your dress is so beautiful.'

'Thank you,' said Lara.

She hadn't been allowed to look at herself in a mirror with the dress on—apparently another Sicilian tradition. But she'd had her mother's dress adjusted slightly so that it fitted her perfectly.

It was classically simple and sweetly bohemian, with its high neck and ruffled bodice. She wore her hair down and a garland of flowers adorned her head. No veil. She didn't need to hide any more—from anything.

Isabella pressed a simple bouquet of local flowers into her hands and then stepped in front of her to start her walk down the aisle.

Roberto, her twin brother, was acting as groomsman to Ciro. And Lazaro was there too—Ciro's best friend. His eyes had been suspiciously shiny earlier, when they'd had an informal pre-ceremony lunch.

He'd taken Lara's hands and said, 'I'm sorry for doubting you.'

Lara had shaken her head and said, 'No need to apologise. I'm glad you were there for him.'

Lazaro had grimaced. 'He wasn't a pretty

sight the day you got married the first time. I had to peel him off the floor of a bar—'

'Filling my wife's head with stories again, Lazaro?'

Lara had smiled and put her hand over Ciro's, where his arm had wrapped around her waist, leaning back against him and revelling in his solid strength and love. He'd told her about how he'd gone out and got blind drunk the day of her wedding to Henry Winterborne.

She knew everything. And so did he. No more secrets.

Now she hesitated for a moment on the threshold of the small chapel. Hovering between the past and present. Ciro hadn't turned to look at her walk down the aisle at their first wedding ceremony, but even as that thought formed in her head he turned around now.

And even though she hadn't been allowed to look at herself in her wedding dress, she didn't need to. She could see herself reflected in his eyes as she walked towards him and she'd never felt more beautiful or more desired.

Or more loved.

She was home. At last.

Hours later, after the revelry had finally died down and Ciro had picked her up to carry her to their suite amidst much catcalling and cheering, Lara stood facing out to where the dawn was breaking on a new day on the horizon.

Ciro was behind her, undoing each tiny button on the dress—undressing his bride to make love to her, kissing each sliver of exposed skin.

Lara's eyes filled with tears. She whispered, 'I dreamt of this moment but I never dared to believe it might come true. I was so scared to love again after losing my family.'

Ciro's hands stopped and he turned her around to face him. He wiped her tears away. 'It's not a dream…it's real. Because you were brave enough to trust.'

Lara smiled through her tears. 'Because you made me fall for you.'

Ciro smiled smugly. 'That too.'

Then his smile faded and he put a hand to her belly between them. 'And we can have more too, if you trust me.'

She whispered, 'A family…'

He nodded. 'I wouldn't want this with anyone else. Only you.'

'Me too.'

'Let's start now. This morning.'

Lara reached up and put her arms around his neck, pressing her mouth to his before saying emotionally, 'Yes, please.'

Nine months later, in a hospital in Palermo, Ciro and Lara welcomed a baby son—Carlo—and their family was complete.

At least until Margarita arrived a couple of years later.

And then Stefano.

Then it was complete.

* * * * *